DATE DUE

JUN 0 1 1995	JUL 1 9 2003
FEB 0 2 1996	
NOV 2 7 1996 APR 1 7 1997	
JUL 1 2 1997	
SEP 2 4 1997	
DEC 2 3 1997	
FEB 2 3 1998	
APR 0 5 1999	
JUN 2 4 1999	
JUL 1 2 1999	
NOV 2 5 2000 JAN 2 5 2001	
MAR 1 6 2002	
APR 1 9 2002	

DEMCO 38-297

FOOTNOTE
TO
MURDER

FOOTNOTE
TO
MURDER

L. A. Taylor

 ————————————————

Walker and Company ✳ New York

I'm just not bloodthirsty enough for this, Marge told herself. It's even worse than I thought it would be.

Shifting her weight on the straight wooden chair, she continued to read, bottom lip caught under her teeth. She turned the page, index card in hand—she had switched to five-by-eights for this job, just for this purpose—ready to slap the card over any gruesome illustration that might appear, before she had a chance to look at it too closely.

The next two pages were blessedly pictureless. Marge stretched her long, jeans-clad legs under the table, yawned, and let her gaze wander over the reading room. The usual Wednesday morning assortment of other readers was dotted about the room: a few elderly men and women with shopping bags beside their chairs, a couple of students, a woman who looked like a suburban housewife on her first trip to the main city library, all preserving their distance from one another with the unspoken agreement of starlings on a telephone wire. Some of them she knew by sight, like the elderly man at the other end of her own table. Too early in the season for the winter drifters who came for the warmth, thank heaven. You never saw the drifters in the university library, Marge mused. That was different, full of kids, livelier even though it was half underground and lacked the distraction of sunlight beckoning through tall windows. It even smelled different: no years of wax were layered on those modern brick floors. And sounded different: no desolate hush seemed to echo from the vaulted ceiling, punctuated only by a footstep, the sibilance of a whisper, the creak of a chair. Marge missed it, but that might only be because she didn't like this job.

Could be worse, Marge, she reminded herself. You could still be working for the insurance company at precisely a nickel an hour above the minimum wage. And you remember how far that goes, divided by four people: nowhere near the end of the month.

Marge wriggled on the seat, folded one leg under her like a woman half her age. She looked back at the book, and her mouth tightened. Why would anybody in his right mind want to write a whole book about murder? Could that many people want to read such a book?

Apparently, yes. Not only that, to judge from the extent of the library's collection, Mr. Greyborn was just one of a horde who wrote to their taste. Except that he meant to concentrate on unsolved cases. Marge rubbed her fingers across her mouth, as if she had just eaten something rancid, although she hadn't actually eaten anything at all since the single cup of tea she'd had for breakfast. If she had a choice (but, she reminded herself, she didn't), she'd never have taken on this job. Even though she'd really had to scrape to meet this month's rent, she'd almost doubled her rates when Mr. Greyborn phoned her, tempting fate to scare him off. But he hadn't even hesitated before he agreed! Phil must have given her a recommendation and a half.

Well, Marge me lass, she thought, and sighed. If you are going to do free-lance research instead of sitting in the typing pool and still get Peggy through school and the braces on Claire's teeth paid for, you have to take what comes. Even unsolved murders. Her stomach growled in agreement.

She caught her thoughts meandering and reread the two unillustrated pages, her neat shorthand racing across one of the index cards beside her. The next page displayed the gory contents of a trunk, over which Marge slapped the free card. She shrugged off a shudder and, inching the card higher on the page until the caption appeared, read that the trunk had been recovered from a dock in Boston, where it had lain unclaimed in the customs office until its foul odor provoked an investigation. Unlike most people, Marge Brock was not the least bit tempted to peek again at the picture.

She slipped the card to the next page with a practiced flick, telling herself it was just as well she'd decided to economize by skipping lunches this week. A single red hair fell to the page; Marge brushed the hair away with the edge of her hand and started taking notes again.

"Glad to see you so busy on my old man's behalf," a light male voice interrupted.

Marge squinted up at the man across the table. "Phil!" she exclaimed. "What are you doing here?"

"Looking for you."

"Oh." Marge took her reading glasses off and rubbed the bridge of her nose. "Message from your father, or what?" she asked, remembering to drop her voice to a whisper.

"Nothing to do with him." Phil Greyborn put his hands in his pockets and looked down at his feet. "I was sort of hoping I could take you to lunch. Renew an old friendship, that kind of thing."

Marge blinked. "Oh," she said again. Her stomach commented eagerly on the idea of lunch. "I am hungry," she admitted.

"So I hear." Phil's grin transformed his rather plain middle-aged face into something boyish and appealing. Marge smiled back. "Since you're not dressed for the Carleton Room and I can't afford it anyway, how about Jimmy's?"

"I've never been there. What's it like?"

"How long did you say you've lived here?"

"Nine years," Marge said, forgetting to whisper.

"And you've never been to Jimmy's?"

"I don't get around much," Marge explained, gesturing at the scattered note cards and the open book. "What with the kids and all."

Phil leaned on his knuckles on the table. "And here I was thinking all divorcées were supposed to be so—wait a minute, that's not coming out right. Will you come to lunch?" he asked, raising his eyebrows with his inflection. "At Jimmy's? It's a good-food bar."

Marge glanced again at the book and at the sunshine streaming through the leaded-glass windows and let her stomach make the decision. "Sure," she said. "Thanks." She gathered her notes together and tucked them into her briefcase with the books she was working on. "Just let me check all this junk at the desk."

As they passed the other end of the long table, the elderly man who always claimed that seat lifted his head and said "Shhh!" so loudly that every face in the room turned. Marge dropped her head and murmured an apology as she headed for the reference desk. Phil Greyborn, close behind, pushed open one of the big oak doors of the reading room and let her pass through. The door swung shut behind them with a satisfying thud. Marge's breath whooshed out.

"Free at last, hmm?" Phil asked.

"Something like that."

She left the briefcase, trading smiles with the librarian on duty, and they walked down a flight of echoing iron steps to the bronze doors that protected the halls of knowledge from the cold, cruel world of downtown. "It's only a couple of blocks to Jimmy's," Phil said. "I'm parked farther away than that, so we may as well walk."

"Fine," Marge agreed. "If you'll slow down a little."

Phil adjusted his long stride to match hers, half turning as she ran a couple of steps to catch up. At the corner, they stopped beside a young honey-locust tree standing dejectedly in a circle of spike-topped fencing. A few of the lacy leaves drifted to the sidewalk as they waited. A clunk sounded inside a box on a pole beside them, and the green light blinked on.

"Go," said Phil.

❧ II ❧

Lᴜɴᴄʜ-ʜᴏᴜʀ shoppers crowded the street, crossing anywhere along the block; a red bus progressed slowly among them as if breasting a wave. Phil caught Marge's hand to pull her out of its path. She gained the curb opposite a little out of breath and wrinkling her nose against the exhaust fumes.

Outside Jimmy's, she dodged a Hare Krishna and ducked under Phil's arm as he held the door for her. The odor of food, good food, seized her. She swallowed a spurt of saliva and blinked at the semidark until the green afterimage of sunlight on sidewalk faded.

"The pastrami here is great," Phil said. "If you like pastrami." He took her elbow and steered her toward the back of the long room.

"Love it," Marge said.

"I thought so." Phil gestured toward one of the booths. "That is, I thought I remembered that you did."

"After, what? Seventeen years? That's awfully good remembering." She slid onto the black leather bench and regarded him quizzically across the table.

"Food," Phil explained. He patted a somewhat rounded belly and leaned toward her to be heard over the thump of the jukebox. "My big passion. That's what I remember best about people — what they eat. I couldn't tell you anything important about yourself, though. Except that you have a kid — a daughter?"

"Two daughters and a son, as a matter of fact."

The waitress came and tried to push some menus at them, but Phil waved them off. "Two pastrami plates," he ordered. "And I'll have a beer. Marge?"

"Sounds good to me." She hadn't had a beer in a long time, three or four months at least.

"MillerSchlitzLöwenbräu?" demanded the waitress.

"The Miller draft," Phil said. "Okay with you, Marge?"

Marge nodded and the waitress went away. The music blared on, familiar-sounding, although all she could hear was the rhythm.

"How old are your kids?" Phil asked, leaning forward again and pushing the ashtray out of the way.

"Peggy, she's the one you remember, is nineteen. Chuck is going on seventeen, and Claire's twelve."

"Let me guess. You've been divorced five years."

"Six."

"Me, too."

"You were pretty close, though," Marge said. "How did you guess?"

"Timing." Phil spread his hands out on the table. Long, large-jointed hands, Marge noticed, like her father's. "Typical timing. I've noticed it a lot, lately. Me, I was a seven-year man. Charlie was obviously a fifteen-year man, or you wouldn't have the youngest one. Claire."

"He could have been slow," Marge pointed out, a bit annoyed because Phil's guess—the fifteen years—had been right on the button. She didn't like to feel she was living by some unwritten timetable. "Say, ten or eleven years. It happens."

"Not Charlie. Too conventional."

Marge grimaced at the absolute confidence in his voice. Feeling as if something in her had been pushed into place, she looked down at her hands and was surprised to see that she was folding her paper napkin into tiny, even pleats. "No," she agreed, "not Charles." She shook the napkin out and spread it on her lap. "Do you have any kids?"

Phil also looked down, stretched his knobbly fingers again, adjusted his knife and fork. "Not anymore."

Marge waited, but he said nothing more. "Do I ask?" she ventured after several seconds.

"Crib death. A girl, Jessica. Three months old."

Marge winced. "I'm sorry."

"I was baby-sitting," Phil said without raising his head. Marge leaned forward to hear him. "That's what broke us up, really. Sharon always blamed me. Something I did, something I didn't do. Either way, my fault. It took a while to come to a head, but that's what did it." He moved the water glass a quarter inch. "People didn't know as much about it then as they do now."

"No." Marge looked past him, to the plastic greenery separating their booth from the next. "I was spared that, at least."

"And it all blew up when Pop was visiting, to make it worse," Phil said, sighing. He twitched a smile at her. "Let's talk about something else. I know you were at Oxford and at Harvard when I was, with Charlie. Then where did you go?"

Marge almost giggled. "Oh, you'd never believe. Lawrence, Kansas. A suburb of Dallas, or something, all country music and cowboy boots. Incredible! Like a foreign country, compared to Boston. You can imagine how that sat with Charles. And you?"

"Missouri. Not quite as far west, but they thought it was. Then you moved here?"

"Uh-uh." Marge shook her head, smiling again. "We had a bad habit of moving every time I got pregnant. Next stop was Ohio —Cleveland. That's where Charlie quit teaching. He didn't get tenure, so he resigned and got a job selling computers. The company transferred him, and here I am."

"You know, that's quite a coincidence," Phil remarked. "I spent a couple of years in Akron, myself."

"That's what? Thirty miles from Cleveland? Parallel routes," Marge commented. "When was that?"

"Oh, ten years ago, maybe."

"What are you doing now?"

"Teaching at St. Anne's. Pop calls it St. Podunk's. He's right, too. The only one-room college in the upper Midwest. Fortunately, it's completely surrounded by the university. Classics, of course."

"That's right." Marge nodded as the pastrami plate, two slabs of dark rye bread piled with pink strips of meat and surrounded by potato salad and spears of dull green pickle, was set in front of her. "Good grief," she said. "I'm not sure I can eat all that."

"Put a little meat on your bones," Phil said as he tucked pickle into his pastrami and put the second slab of bread on top. "Won't hurt you. Where's our beer?"

Marge glanced at the bar, saw the waitress pick up two overflowing mugs and turn toward them. "She's bringing it now."

"Good," Phil said, muffled by the sandwich.

Marge regarded him thoughtfully. "You haven't changed much," she said. "Hair a little thinner, face not quite so thin, but

I'd have recognized you even if you hadn't stopped me that day."

"Oh, no, you wouldn't've," Phil said, chuckling. "You had your head down and you were *charging*. I had to look around to make sure no dragons had invaded the university library."

"Not dragons," Marge said and laughed. "Seventeenth-century feminists, if such a breed existed. People write about the damndest things."

"Dragons," Phil repeated. He intercepted his beer on its way to the table and took a sip. "Just as I thought. Lucky thing I saw you, St. Georgina."

"What? Oh, yeah. Lucky for me, anyway," Marge said. "Thanks for recommending me to your father," she added, to be polite.

"My pleasure. I was supposed to be on the lookout for a good researcher. Those girls at St. Podunk's are still trying to figure out whether English reads left to right or right to left."

His mouth screwed into an expression so sour, Marge had to laugh. "It can't be as bad as all that," she protested.

"It can, oh, it can." Phil took a long swallow of beer. "You'd be astonished at what comes out of high schools these days. No, not astonished. The right word is appalled."

"It must have taken some nerve to give me a good recommendation after all this time, all the same."

Phil, still holding his sandwich, rested his wrists on the edge of the table without taking a bite. "People don't change much, Marge. You always were a careful scholar."

"How would you know?" Marge cocked her head at him, puzzled. "I never even met you until after I graduated."

"You don't think anybody ever believed Charlie wrote his papers himself, do you?" He laughed at her raised eyebrows. "Oh, come on, Marge. Charlie may be the original Mr. Nice Guy, but he's not all that bright."

"He—"

"Okay, okay." Phil made shushing motions, grabbed at a chunk of pickle that fell from his sandwich, missed. "Bright isn't really what I mean. Bright he is, I give you that. But lazy. Not capable of sitting down to work. That had to be you."

Marge made a face at the potato salad.

"Well," Phil said, "anyway, I didn't mind recommending you to Pop. Happy to, as I said."

She smiled faintly. "Thanks." The word came out louder than she had expected, in the pause between two jukebox numbers, startling her. The music came back, even louder but with a slower beat, as she started on the potato salad. She was shocked at how hungry she had been; the tang of the mayonnaise almost brought tears to her eyes. They ate in silence for several minutes, until the music stopped again. Phil cleared his throat.

"You don't like this job much, do you?" he asked. "I mean, this particular one, for my father."

Marge shrugged. "It's a job."

"I was watching you, watching your face for a couple of minutes, back at the library, before I said anything. What's with the index card?"

"Oh." Marge felt herself blush, touched a finger to her cheek. "It's so I won't have to look at the pictures."

"Murder's that bad, hmm?"

"I don't even like to think about it," she admitted. "I can't see how people can do it. Angry as I've sometimes been..." She paused, remembering how angry she had sometimes been. Screaming angry. Numb angry. Scared angry. "...and writing books about it..."

"Ghoulish?"

She looked down at her plate, was surprised to see she'd eaten everything. "Yeah, sort of."

"But you don't want to say so, because it's my father."

"Phil—" She tipped her head, embarrassed.

"Everything all right here?" asked the waitress.

"Yes."

"Got everything you want?"

"Yes." Firmly, in unison.

The woman slapped the bill down between them, and Phil watched her head for the next booth. "Don't worry," he said. "I'm used to it. People can't seem to keep writers separated from what they write about, and when you've got a father who makes his living writing true-crime books, you take a lot of flak."

Marge laughed, a nervous titter she cut short.

"He's not a bad man to work for," Phil continued. "And he has absolutely no murderous tendencies, in case you're worried."

"It never even occurred to me," she protested, shocked.

"Relax, I was teasing." Phil picked up the bill and reached into his hip pocket for his wallet. "Tell me about your kids."

She did, while he paid the bill and rummaged in his pocket for the tip, and through the walk back to the library, and for five minutes standing on the outside steps, until she saw a man hurry past with a glance at his watch and looked at her own. "Whoops, two o'clock," she said. "I'd better get back to work. I get paid by the hour, you know."

"Add in the time for lunch."

She glanced down at him. He was standing three steps below her, looking up as if searching for something. Phil was a pleasant-faced man, attractive in a way, with wispy brown hair and round hazel eyes. The fifteen or so extra pounds on his tall frame softened his jawline slightly. He grinned at her. "I couldn't do that, Phil," she said. "You know I couldn't do that."

The grin broadened. "Marge, you're too honest," Phil said, his voice warm. "Don't expect everybody to be like you—there's a whole big world out here, just full of people waiting to take advantage of sweet things like you."

"I think Charles taught me that," she said bleakly.

Phil looked away. "Sorry," he mumbled. "I forgot. Well, thanks for letting me take you to lunch. When do you see Pop again?"

"Thursday afternoon. Oh, gosh, that's tomorrow. I really ought to be done with the British by then." She went up two more steps. "Thanks for lunch. But I'm not going to charge the time to your father."

He shook his head slightly, smiling to himself. "No double dipping, hey? Well, I'll see you, Marge." He sketched a wave and turned away, looking oddly gawky despite the extra weight, much like the graduate student she remembered from, what? Almost half her life ago.

"Phil," she called after him, on impulse. "It was fun."

But he didn't hear. He walked on, looking younger than his years in his jeans and joggers, clothes none of them would have dreamed of wearing downtown when she'd known him last. She wondered why she hadn't thought of that sooner.

As she waited to retrieve her briefcase from the desk, Marge remembered standing, waiting for Charles, in the Bodleian

Library at Oxford, so many years before. She hadn't been a student, not officially—that was Charles—so she had been confined to an anteroom, to look at a small glass case in which a tiny portrait of Percy Bysshe Shelley had been displayed for months on end, the only morsel she recalled of one of the greatest libraries in the world. How she had longed to walk past that inner door!

She steeled herself to go back to work with the memory of the bill the orthodontist had sent the week before and got out her cards, found her place in the book. By three-thirty, the index card was flipping over each new page with a proficient little snap, and the case histories were flowing in at her eyes and out at her pencil point with minimal participation from her brain. She had started a new book by then, not so profusely illustrated as the last had been, and after several pages of pictureless text she grew careless.

But the picture she missed covering was only a sketch of a noose, just a drawing, perfectly safe to look at. Marge snickered as she read the caption. The British might have puzzled over that knot, but she didn't. Her father had tied up the boat with it hundreds of times. Maritime occupation? Hah! Dad had never set oar into any body of water he couldn't see all shores of at once. Cheered by feeling one up, Marge read this case with more attention than the others.

"Why, I was there!" she exclaimed aloud, stunned. The old man at the other end of the table pierced the room with his "Shhh!" but she hardly heard him. Could she be right?

Casting back, oh, twenty years, to that longing on the steps of the old stone library... how young she had been! On the other end of things, then, writing from somebody else's notes, Charles's infuriating, sketchy notes. Married two years, Peggy only months away, Charles conning the world with her writing. The blush flared again: conning *some* of the world with her writing. She hadn't had time to read newspapers, hadn't had a taste for crime news even if she had read them, and she and Charles had never stretched the fellowship money to cover the cost of a radio—a wireless—and the license to own one. So she hadn't known about this string of deaths.

But the date was exactly right. Marge shuddered. Women

leaving country pubs, not far from Oxford, set upon and strangled by someone who used this sort of noose, tied in a nylon stocking from Marks and Spencer. She passed her left hand uneasily over her thigh. Her own stockings had come from Marks, then. Had she stood next to a murderer at the counter, perhaps? She lifted her hands to smooth down the hair at the back of her neck and knocked the stack of note cards to the floor with her shirt sleeve. The elderly man who had held down the other end of the table all day got up and stamped out. Marge barely noticed.

She picked up the cards and sorted and stacked them slowly and precisely. Probably an American, she mentally informed the puzzled author of the book. Tying what was probably a Boy Scout knot. The woods around Oxford—well, the pubs, anyway—had been full of American Boy Scout types in 1961 and '62. Marge sighed, turned the page with improvident breeziness, and was confronted by a clear, sharp photo of one of Jack the Ripper's victims. She pounced on it with the card. Nightmare city.

I'd better mark that last case to follow up, she thought, closing the book. It was still unsolved as of the publication of this collection, in 1979. As were the Whitechapel murders, of course, but Mr. Greyborn had said he was looking for cases that hadn't been written up very often, and even Marge had heard of Jack the Ripper.

Time to quit. She was getting fuzzy-headed. That beer she'd had for lunch, most likely.

Twenty minutes later, Marge was walking down the granite steps of the library with the gritty wind of freedom blowing into her face. No more murder until nine the next morning, and in her briefcase, an old Erma Bombeck to bring her back to normal for the evening.

And she thinks she's in the pits, thought Marge.

❊ III ❊

Her schedule wasn't working out. Marge pushed at the short, wavy hair over her ear with the eraser end of her pencil. Two more days on the British, she calculated, eyeing the thickness of the lower book in the pile of two, before she could even begin on the Americans. And Greyborn to meet this afternoon. She took a last glance at the sunny, round-topped windows of the reading room and opened the book she had started the day before, feeling somewhat harried.

Not that she could work up any regret about the time spent on yesterday's lunch. A jukebox rhythm sounded faintly, quite unbidden, in her mind. Odd. The memories the sight of Phil Greyborn had brought back had kept her awake most of the night: Charles and his who-knew-how-many affairs, conducted out of town, where he didn't even have to lie. A girl in every port. Every major city, anyway. Marge slid down in the chair without finding a comfortable position, not because of the shock of her finding out about Charles, strong even only remembered, or even because of the way she had found out. What made her squirm, Marge had to admit, was just that the whole business made her feel so stupid! Because, in retrospect, any lummox ought to have known the man was lying.

All nice-guy charm, that was Charles. Part of what made him a good salesman. Marge sighed, then shifted again on the hard oak seat. Not that she ever saw any of that fantastic money he claimed to be making, now that he'd left academia behind. Support payments did show up, few and far between. Six years of inflation had made the court-ordered figure a bad joke, anyway. Cost more to sue for than she'd get out of it.

Memories that scalded, yes, but she couldn't very well hold them against Phil Greyborn, with his open face and his habit of standing just a little pigeon-toed, with his weight flat on one foot and on the outside of the other.

Charles moved more on the balls of his feet. And would, any day now. She could feel it coming. He'd move, on the balls of his unerring feet, straight up the stairs to her apartment. He always showed up when she was feeling least able to face him. Or was it just that she felt worst when she guessed he was about to arrive? He was about due, she reflected.

The elderly man who owned the other end of the table claimed his place, and Marge shook herself, like a dog coming in from the rain, and began reading.

By the time she pulled the peanut butter sandwich Peggy had made for her that morning out of her briefcase to start a clandestine lunch, she was feeling more her normal, not-so-introspective self. The elderly man cleared his throat, but she paid no attention. Eating in the library was against the rules. So? He did it himself, and Marge had seen him. She stifled an urge to thumb her nose and kept eating.

The book she had started earlier that morning was much like the others she'd read, with much the same collection of cases, and she'd been able to skim and leave out the note-taking, except for an odd detail here and there. Marge's memory was her strength: she prided herself on it; in the long night hours she exercised it the way other people exercise their muscles. Let facts demolish demons.

She was sure when she came across something the other books had left out: details, mostly, her confident pencil noting the misspellings in Jack the Ripper's note to Scotland Yard, the red hair of all the Oxfordshire victims, the address label on the Boston trunk. All grist for Mr. Greyborn's mill, may he grind merrily, she thought. To her horror, the gorgeous Granny Smith apple she'd found in her briefcase cracked like a falling tree as she bit into it. People three tables away raised their heads and stared at her, and the elderly man not only scowled, he actually shook his finger at her.

She dropped her hand, the apple, and her gaze into her lap and tried to chew without making any noise, ears burning. She finished the book with her lunch and turned to the last, fattest book, determined to register at least a small start before leaving to meet Mr. Greyborn.

Bonanza! No chapter notes. Without sources to check, the book was useless. She skimmed over the table of contents anyway, saw no cases she hadn't encountered before, and wrote out a card to show she'd reviewed the book. Then it was time, past time, to pull her things together and get going. She gave the elderly man her very sweetest smile on her way out. He sniffed. His nose, long, straight, and aristocratic, was perfectly suited to the purpose.

The weather had changed overnight. Still sunny but cooler, a real autumn day with a wind that went right through the linen weave of the dress Marge had put on in honor of her appointment. Even standing in the bus shelter, where the wind was at least baffled, she almost wished she had worn a sweat shirt instead. Naturally, the bus came late, and she shivered as she climbed the steps, dropped her coins into the box, and held out her hand for a transfer.

She plunked into a seat and started to page through her transcribed notes, stopping now and then to add a detail or a reference gleaned from the morning's reading. Not the best-organized job she'd ever done, but probably adequate. Marge re-sorted the pages with a dissatisfied grimace. Twenty-three sufficiently gory cases, eight or ten of which might fit Mr. Greyborn's criteria: relatively recent, relatively unknown, unsolved.

Where had the apple come from?

She stashed the completed notes in her briefcase and stared out the window, watching for her stop. Peggy must have bought apples. Peggy was the fruit lover in the family; it wouldn't be the first time she'd spent some of her earnings on fruit, even though Marge was careful to balance their meals. Still, the things cost over thirty cents apiece. A good kid, Peggy. A good kid, by which Marge meant helpful, uncomplaining.

She shivered again as she walked the two blocks to Greyborn's office. He had what the landlord called a "suite" in an old Victorian house, one of those clapboard and shingle monsters a prospective turn-of-the-century homeowner could order by mail and have delivered, precut, with all of its gingerbread ready for assembly. Marge tried to imagine the horse-drawn lumber wagon straining up the hill to the site. Dust everywhere, and saplings where these hefty lindens now stood. Why couldn't she be researching something like that? Old pictures at the historical society; the pleasant, musty paper of old magazines. Although, she thought, sighing, she'd probably end up at the historical society yet, looking for old murders.

The house had started out as a duplex but was now divided

into several offices, of which Greyborn's was the first floor left front. Across the rather dark hall, the Bellflower Press threatened to spill its stacked manuscripts onto the scratched parquet of the entrance, while two young men screamed at each other about somebody's poetry. Marge listened for a moment and decided she was glad it wasn't hers.

"Mrs. Brock?" the secretary asked as Marge pushed open Greyborn's outer door. "Oh, shut the door, quick!" the secretary said. "Those two are having another editorial conference, and I just can't stand it."

"Is that what they call it?"

"So I hear. Mr. Greyborn will be so glad to see you," the secretary rushed on. "He's a little pressed for time this afternoon, and he was hoping you wouldn't be late. Now, here you are ten minutes early!" The secretary, a woman perhaps ten years older than herself whose name Marge didn't know, rewarded her with a pleased smile, then bustled across the tiny reception room and stuck her head through Mr. Greyborn's doorway. Marge stood uneasily, wondering if she should sit down.

"Imagistic crap!" bellowed a voice in the hall. The door of Bellflower Press slammed mightily, followed by the house door. Something rattled inside the walls.

"Oh, good," said the secretary. "They're through. Mr. Greyborn will see you right away."

Marge went frowning into the inner office, shook Greyborn's extended hand, and sat in the comfortable armchair at the corner of Greyborn's desk.

"Something troubling you, Mrs. Brock?"

"Not really." Marge smiled briefly. "It's just the—ah—editorial conference across the hall."

"Oh, yes. I heard the plaster coming down," Greyborn said, his face utterly without expression. "They must have reached an agreement."

"Agreement?"

"Two slammed doors seems to constitute an agreement. Perhaps I should say, a capitulation. What have you got for me?"

"Quite a bit." Marge pulled her notes out of her briefcase and passed them across the desk. "A lot of this is pretty old stuff. Jack the Ripper and Dr. Cream."

"That's solved, anyway."

"I know. I've got eight I'm pretty sure are what you're looking for, though, and two possibilities. They're the ones on top."

Greyborn took the sheets of paper and began to read, sucking at his lips. Marge looked at the room. On her last visit, she'd been too taken up with getting her assignment right to look at the room very closely. A nice room, she decided, tall, lined with white-painted bookshelves containing dictionaries, atlases, an encyclopedia, and an assortment of other books she didn't recognize, including a small group with bright dust jackets. *Pulling It Off*, she read sideways, *The Story of a Heist*. George Greyborn was the author. The others must be his, too.

She studied the man as he leafed through her notes a second time. Tall, slender, he had to be in his late sixties—after all, he was Phil's father, and Phil must be in his middle forties; he was her own age. But George Greyborn didn't look that old, despite his white hair. Sidelit by the bay window of his office, he looked distinguished, a gentleman. More like an athletic senator than a crime writer.

"Oh, wonderful," he said suddenly, looking up with an eager grin. "Oh, superb! You've got a couple here I didn't know about myself, and I'd already done a little reading when I hired you. The Oxfordshire ones, and this case in Manchester. Bizarre, that one. And what's this one in Liverpool?"

"That's pretty unclear," Marge conceded. "It was just a side reference in one of the other cases. Pretty old, too: 1917."

"A little outside my range, unless it turns out to be unusually interesting," Greyborn agreed. "But these do look very good, as preliminaries. I can't wait to see what you find on this side of the ocean."

"I was wondering..." Marge began.

Greyborn jutted his chin at her. Marge wondered if Phil would have that chin if he were as thin as his father. Greyborn's nostrils flared, a hound on the scent, and Marge's resolution faltered. She swallowed and pushed on.

"Could I put off starting on the Americans until next week? I'm getting, um, a little burned out."

Greyborn nodded and sucked at his lips. "Phil warned me that you were a little, shall we say, delicate of mind. Do you

[21]

really need the rest? You could get in another day and a half this week." He nodded as he spoke, urging agreement.

"Well…"

"I have a firm deadline from my publisher," he added. "And this is the first time I haven't concentrated on a single case. I'd like to allow myself as much time as possible to make my selections and decide how to organize the book."

Marge hesitated a few seconds. "I don't know," she said finally, without meaning to dicker.

Greyborn's forehead knotted so fiercely that the silver hair on his temples moved forward into two fans. "What if I raised your pay, say ten percent? Would that keep you going?"

Ten percent more would make a little better than double her usual fee. Marge swallowed again. Maybe I just haven't been charging enough, she thought, and nodded.

"Good, good. I'll tell Miss Turki."

So that was the secretary's name.

"Oh, has she given you your check for last week yet?" Greyborn asked. "Pick it up on your way out, then," he said when she shook her head. "Buy yourself a sweater."

Marge's jaw dropped.

"Your arms. They're covered with goosebumps." He picked up a pen and nodded at her, and Marge went into the outer office, where Miss Turki handed her the check. Two hundred eleven beautiful smackeroos. She put it in her purse without even kissing it and headed home.

Peggy met her at the apartment door, eating another of the Granny Smith apples. "Dad called," she said, chewing. "He's in town, or he's going to be in town, or something. He'll call back later, he said."

"Oh, marvelous," Marge groaned. "Just what I needed."

"That's a nice attitude."

Marge ignored the comment and set the briefcase down just inside the door. She rubbed her cold arms. "Thanks for the apple, Peggy," she said.

"De nada," Peggy replied, taking another bite of the one in her hand. "I figured you could use it."

"Thanks," Marge repeated. "Where is everybody?"

"Claire's over at Stevenson's, baby-sitting. She'll have supper there and be home by nine-thirty. Chuck's around somewhere." Peggy headed for the kitchen.

Marge poked her head into the living room, saw Chuck sprawled in front of the TV. "Have you got your homework done, young man?" she inquired.

"Yeah." Chuck didn't move. Marge went into the kitchen, glanced at Peggy's books and papers spread out on the worn Formica tabletop, peered into the refrigerator with a worried frown.

"When do you have to be at work?" she asked Peggy.

"Six. I've got a few minutes yet, before I have to go. I'll grab a burger there." Peggy started to gather up the books.

"Have something green before you go, okay?" Marge said. "I'll warm up some of yesterday's casserole for me and Chuck, if he hasn't eaten it yet," she decided. "Is there any lettuce left?"

"There was an hour ago." Peggy stopped stacking her papers and started to read one. "Oh-oh. This is going to take a shade more work," she said, sitting down. "Did that guy pay you anything today?"

"Uh-huh." Marge fished a pickle out of a jar and closed the refrigerator door.

"You don't sound real excited about it."

"I can't get all that gore out of my mind," Marge explained. She watched Peggy open a book and glance from book to paper. "I wish I hadn't taken the idiot job."

"Can't you get out of it?" Peggy asked, scribbling.

"Not now. Not with Claire's teeth."

"Get Dad to pay for them."

Marge snorted, all the reply the suggestion deserved, and ate the pickle.

Peggy glanced up at her from under her eyebrows, a little trick that was all that was left of Charles. The eyebrows themselves, the wide-set blue eyes, the auburn hair, the freckles, even the triangular chin, were Marge's. "I could take on a few more hours at McDonald's," she offered.

"No." Marge smiled at her daughter, was surprised to feel the sting of tears in her eyes. Good Lord, I'm tired of all this, she thought. "You need the time to study, and besides, it wouldn't

[23]

begin to make up for the pay on this one." Marge sighed, trying to do arithmetic in her head. "I really boxed myself in on that."

"Well." Peggy tapped her pencil against her front teeth. "It's only preliminaries, isn't it? He's not going to have you go dig out all the original references?"

"Oh, no! He'll do all that himself. This is just so he can pick out the good ones. I hope," she added, with visions of yards of microfilmed documents to be examined, the unsettling details of police reports to be digested.

"It can't last too long, then," Peggy said, writing again.

"No." But it was already too long. Nine lousy days and she was sick of it, even getting smudgy blue shadows under her eyes from the bad dreams. Cultivate a little academic detachment, Marge, she told herself as she took the casserole out of the refrigerator and put it into the oven to warm. She reinvestigated the refrigerator, found the limp remaining lettuce, and began to shred it. Nothing else saladable in the house, alas, and two days before she'd have time to shop.

After dinner, she changed into her flannel nightgown and robe and settled down in the old rocker in the girls' bedroom to read, while Chuck went back to the television. Claire came in only ten minutes late, before Marge had a chance to work up a full case of worry. A few minutes later, she evicted her son from the living room and opened the couch out into her bed.

The ten-o'clock news came on almost immediately. Much the same as any night: first a disaster, in this case a wreck on the freeway. The nightly murder: a young man in South Dakota had potted his grandmother with a deer rifle. Greyborn ought to be able to write his book straight out of the daily newspaper, Marge thought. Tax cuts, spending cuts, the unbalanced local, state, and federal budgets. A small foreign war, and a cut to a tortilla chip commercial. Crunch.

The phone rang just as the neat young man with the walrus moustache began his lecture on meteorological systems. Charles? Marge considered not answering. But possibly Peggy. She climbed out of bed and headed for the kitchen.

"Marge? Phil Greyborn."

She blinked with surprise. "Hi, Phil."

"I didn't wake you, did I?"

"No, no. I was just watching the news."

"Oh. Sorry." Marge had the impression of an uncomfortable pacing at the other end of the line. "Did you see my father today?"

"Yes, I did. Something wrong?" Somebody had left the margarine out of the refrigerator. Marge stretched the phone cord to its limit and put away the margarine with one hand.

"No, no. I was just curious."

"Phil, what's the matter?"

"Nothing's the matter." He sounded irritated. "I just wanted to ask whether you would like to go to a party with me. Not a fancy one," he added, the words tumbling over one another. "And you'll know some of the people there—a couple of the guys who were at Oxford and in Boston later on, and their wives. I was invited, and I asked if I could bring a date."

"Well, I—"

"Kevin Lindstrom, remember him? Wife named Julie?"

"Yes." Pictures of two very young faces sprang up in Marge's mind. "I remember them. Named their daughter Pallas Athena?"

"That's them." Phil sounded pleased. "Theenie, they call her. She just got married herself. Kevin and Julie are giving the party. Marcus Dellingham will be there. He's got a new wife, you won't know her, but Marcus is the same old Marcus. He had a fling with the theater and is back in the academic fold."

Marge was still coping with the idea of the chubby toddler she remembered, getting married.

"I'm sorry, I don't really—I mean," Phil sounded more flustered by the second, "if you have a steady date, that is, I never—"

"It's okay, Phil," Marge said. "Yes, I think I'd like to come."

His relief, even over the wire, was comical. "Oh, good. I'm going to spring you on them, if that's okay by you—our good friend Marge Brock, tossed up by the waves of circumstance upon our beach, that kind of thing."

"Gee, and I thought you'd invited me for my company," Marge teased.

"Oh, I didn't mean—damn it, Marge, I'm just no good at asking for dates, I guess."

She smoothed his ruffled feathers, one eye on the television through the living-room door. Cold again tomorrow, she saw. "Phil, now that I think of it, I wanted to ask you something."

"Shoot."

[25]

"When we were all at Oxford, do you remember hearing about a series of murders in the area?"

"Murders?"

"I ran across them when I was looking for stuff for your father. Stranglings, they were. Do you remember anything like that?"

A long pause.

"Phil?"

"No." He sounded far away. "No, I don't recall anything like that. I don't have my old man's taste for crime."

"Doesn't matter." Marge shrugged, even though he couldn't see her. "I don't remember them myself, either, but I'm sure he'll dig the details out."

"You've told him about it, then."

"Of course," she said, surprised at his flat tone.

"Well. About that party. It's this coming Sunday, is that okay? I'll pick you up about seven. Don't get dressed up, it's just a back-porch deal."

"Sunday at seven," Marge said. "See you then." She hung up with an amused little smile for her warm, happy feeling. A date. The first in how long? She didn't want to think. Ages!

She padded back down the hall in her bare feet, turned the TV off, and climbed back into bed to work the cryptogram from the morning newspaper—disappointingly easy today. Not until she was settled with the lights out did she wonder why Phil would ask whether she'd told his father about that string of long-ago killings. A funny thing for him to care about.

She remembered him in a pub on Iffley Road: He had had thicker hair then and a habit of brushing it off his forehead before he spoke—not often. He'd been shy then, and skinny. A lot of their crowd, most of them Americans, a couple of Germans, and the odd Englishman, used to gather at that pub. Reached by a path among cow pats. Flashlights required.

As the bed warmed, Marge thought of faces, tried to remember names. The Lindstroms, Kevin tipping an occasional mouthful of beer into little Athena to keep her quiet. Marcus Dellingham hadn't been part of that bunch, though she remembered him, too, from lunches at a place near the Bodley. In Ship Street, was it? A short, dark Englishman named Tony. Two Germans,

Karl and Gustav. A woman, Gwen something, with her tag-along husband who seemed to inhabit some world of his own. Dick Green: Was he or wasn't he? And others, that guy who used to sing every blessed verse of "The Star-Spangled Banner" along about nine-thirty and have to be helped to the loo, that blond older man with the tic in his cheek...

Faces that had reappeared in her life from time to time, as one recommended another for a job that had just opened up, or was sought out for the reputation he had with his friends. Ohl, that was Karl's last name. And Tony was Antony Owens; Welsh, not English. Hadn't she seen him at that last convention she'd gone to, in New York? Or had it been in Washington that year?

Finally putting them all out of her mind, Marge stretched and fell into a light sleep, one ear automatically cocked for Peggy's return.

❧IV❧

MURDER in Boston, again.

Not a body packed in a trunk this time, though. Marge watched the peaceful drift of dust through the late-afternoon sunlight. Her mouth felt odd, strained, as she let her mind drift, too, trying to pin down the reason for the faint chill she had felt while reading this latest case. The walls of the reading room had been painted light blue above the walnut bookshelves. Someone had painstakingly preserved the decorations an earlier, more affluent library board had caused to adorn the walls, a frieze of books and flowers. Against the sunlight they looked dim, uncertain.

Marge turned her attention to the few others in the room: three of the regulars and one boy who looked about fifteen. The old man had already left the other end of her table. Most of the chairs were empty, pushed carelessly toward the tables. Somebody had left the paperbound volumes of the *Readers' Guide to Periodical Literature* strewn beside their rack, one of them split open and faced down. Marge resisted the urge to tidy. She looked back down at the book she had been reading.

The sketch of the noose wasn't the same as the one in the book of British murders, but the knot was, only it was drawn from a different angle. Marge wished she had the nerve to take the sketch around the room and show it to everyone there: Can you tie this knot? Something like that. What would they think, that old lady, that kid, that saggy-faced man with the rimless glasses?

You are being ridiculous, she told herself. Everybody must know how to tie a knot like this one.

The author of this book rambled on about Boston as an international port, too. What was this maritime fixation? True, Marge couldn't remember going into downtown Boston without seeing some kind of sailor in uniform, but even so...

She ticked off the other resemblances. The women had all had red hair. They had been raped. Except for what was necessary to accomplish that, they were still clothed. They had all been robbed. They had been strangled with a noose like this one, tied in a nylon stocking. The stockings were a nothing brand, they could have been bought in any supermarket, just like the ones used in Oxford could have been bought at any Marks and Spencer, anywhere in Britain. You could tell he was no gentleman, Marge thought, her mouth compressed into a smirk. He didn't prefer Haynes.

She put her face into her hands, fingers under her reading glasses, and sighed. What is the matter with you? she chided. Jokes, over twelve women dead! The job must be getting to me.

One of the Boston victims had been barely eighteen years old, younger than Peggy was now. Marge stiffened. If she'd had any reason to go up Massachusetts Avenue into Somerville, she might have been one of them herself! But she'd never taken the bus even as far as Porter Square, although Julie Lindstrom had once driven her to the Star Market there. Marge found herself squeezing her earlobes between her thumbs and the knuckles of her forefingers. One of these women had had her heavy gold earrings torn out of her pierced ears. Pierced ears hadn't been so common in '64, '65. She'd never had hers done, herself.

Marge tried to turn the page, but the sketch drew her eye back, and the speculations she'd been trying to push under bubbled out.

She'd been there for these, too. Remembered them, even. A bunch of cases never traced to the Boston Strangler—too different in style, or something. A clear picture of the newsstand in Harvard Square rose up behind her closed lids. Bright magazine covers hanging from clips on a clothesline, stacks of out-of-town newspapers, her own old navy-blue sweater drawn closer as she paused on her way to Mount Auburn Street to read the breathless headlines in the *Globe*. She had shuddered as she read, and shuddered now, as if the wind laden with crumpled candy wrappers that had swirled around the subway entrance touched her still. That was where the chill had come from, she decided.

Could it be coincidence, with so much the same? She couldn't leave the idea alone. One man could easily have done all the murders, these and the ones near Oxford: she could count over a dozen men herself who had been in both places at the right time. There must be hundreds! Students, faculty...as for non-academics, she didn't know about that, but it was surely possible.

And, she reminded herself, it was not only equally possible, but much more likely, that it was all a coincidence.

"Five-thirty, Mrs. Brock," the reference librarian said gently. "We're closing now. Have a nice weekend."

"Oh!" Marge slammed the book shut. "Thanks. You, too." She scrambled her notes together any which way and left.

"I found something funny today." Marge settled her hips against the stub of kitchen counter next to the stove.

Peggy finished tucking papers into books and said, "Mmm?"

"A case in England a few years ago, one they never solved. I read about it a couple of days ago."

"I thought you said today."

The oven timer sounded a stern *ding!* Marge reached for the potholders. "I'm getting to that. This afternoon I ran across another one, just exactly like it, only in Boston." She pulled the hot casserole from the oven and deposited it on the nearest cold burner, turned down the flame under the pot of green beans simmering at the back of the stove.

"Honest?" Peggy finished clearing the table, wiped away something that wasn't the boomerang pattern of the surface, tossed a straw hot pad into the center of it.

Yes, honest, Marge thought irritably. Did you think I'd make it up? Aloud, she said, "It struck me funny."

"What do you mean, just like it?" Peggy asked. "Claire!" she hollered. "Come set the table!"

"Girls, I mean, young women, got strangled."

"Happens," Peggy said distractedly. "You should hear all the warnings we get at work. They've got a deal on karate lessons at the U, by the way. I was thinking I might take them up on it."

"But strangled the same way, with a nylon stocking. Tied with the same kind of knot. It struck me funny," Marge persisted.

"They're five dollars a week, but I think it might be worth it," Peggy said.

"If we can find it," Marge agreed. "Were you listening?"

"Sure." Peggy sounded utterly unimpressed. "Anybody can tie a knot."

"What knot?" Claire asked, making an enormous clatter in the silverware drawer. Chuck walked into the kitchen and without saying a word opened the refrigerator.

"We're just about to eat, Chuck," Marge said.

"Oh, some guy strangled a bunch of women in England," Peggy told Claire.

"With a knot?"

"No, you goop. With a stocking tied in a knot."

Chuck helped himself to a handful of cottage cheese.

"Chuck, for heaven's sake, keep your hands out of the food," Marge remonstrated. "That's for lunch tomorrow, anyway."

"A guy could starve to death."

"So?" Claire asked.

"Your own brother, and you don't even care."

"I was talking to Peggy," Claire flashed, hands on hips.

"So, somebody did it the same way over here. Mom thinks it's funny."

"Ha-ha," Chuck said. "What's funny?"

The telephone rang before anyone replied. Marge snatched up the receiver, hoping for something cheerful. Some pert young thing offering to spray chemicals on the lawn she didn't have, even. She was sorry she'd opened her mouth.

"Hi, honey."

Her shoulders sagged and she brought her stomach under control with an effort. "Hello," she said. A pulse began in her ears.

"It's Dad," Claire informed the rest of them. "Mom's got that socked-sick look she gets."

"I'm in town and I'd like to drop by, if it's not too inconvenient," Charles said, in a tone that suggested to Marge that he'd think any excuse must be trumped up on the spot. "This evening, early, if possible."

"Just a minute." Marge covered the mouthpiece with her palm. "Your father's in town," she said to the kids. "He wants to come see you tonight."

"Oh, crap," Chuck said. "I was going bowling."

"Chuck."

"I promised the guys. And it's my own money. I earned it."
Chuck set his mouth in a stubborn line, just like his father's.

"Is Marylou Smith going bowling, too?" Claire asked with exaggerated interest. Chuck took a mock swing at her. She ducked and stuck out her tongue.

"Chuck has other arrangements," Marge said into the receiver. "But the girls will be here."

"Not me," Peggy said. "I have to be at work at quarter to eight."

"Tell young Charles he doesn't know when he'll see me again and he can cancel his other arrangements." Charles was in a bar. Marge could hear the beat of the jukebox and a lot of loud talk and laughter. She wondered if it were Jimmy's, and she hoped he wasn't drunk.

"I'll tell him," she said. "But I don't know if he'll be here. And Peggy has to work."

"Both of them better be there," Charles said. "Can't you make them? I'll be there in half an hour."

"Charles, Peggy's almost twenty and Chuck's nearly seventeen! How am I going to make them?"

"Just tell them to stay home," he said.

"Charles—"

He hung up. Marge slumped into her chair and began dishing up the casserole. "He'll be here in half an hour," she said. "Can't you stick around a while, Chuck?"

"Good thing it's only half an hour. I wasn't going to leave until seven-thirty, anyway."

Marge glanced at the clock in the back of the stove. Behind the grease-browned glass the hands stood at quarter to seven. "I don't know why he has to do that," she said, more to herself than to anyone else.

"What, is he giving you orders again?" Chuck asked. "'Have your children ready to see me or else!'" he shouted, pounding the table so hard the dishes jumped.

"Chuck, behave yourself."

"You fall for it every time, don't you?" Chuck shoveled green beans into his mouth. "He doesn't want to see us, he just wants a ring in your nose. Thinks it's a big joke to see you run along after him."

The standard words about talking with the mouth full died

on Marge's lips. She stared at her son. Where did a sixteen-year-old learn to make such observations? she asked.

"That's what Peggy says," Chuck mumbled through a mouthful of macaroni. Peggy became extremely interested in what was on her plate. "He'd better be here when he said he would, 'cause I'm not hanging around all night waiting for him to show up."

Marge shrugged helplessly. She looked at the casserole and wondered what had seemed so attractive about the recipe, other than that it was cheap. Yech. "Excuse me," she muttered, standing up. She went into the bathroom to comb her hair and apply a touch of lipstick. Marge, Marge, her reflection said. You're getting old. There's a gray hair, and the freckles on your forehead didn't used to run together like that. She thought of Charles, tall Charles with his razor-ad jaw and muscular shoulders. Although appearances aren't everything, she reminded herself. Not by a long shot.

"What's the use?" she asked the mirror, and wiped the lipstick off. She went into the living room and started to straighten out the afternoon's chaos: folded the morning newspaper, plumped the couch cushions, stacked Chuck's books neatly on the end table. "Whoever had the popcorn can come sweep up!" she yelled. An inarticulate acknowledgment from the kitchen, where the kids were still eating. Marge sat down to wait.

He was ten minutes earlier than he said he'd be, and his hands were full of presents.

Nothing for Marge but a kiss brushed across her cheek that left her heart thudding uncomfortably. He made a small ceremony of presenting each of his children with a slim white box and sat down on the couch with his legs crossed and his arms stretched along the back. Damn him, Marge thought. The sight of him spread out on what was her bed every night turned her stomach.

"Oh, Dad!" Peggy gasped. She held up a gold chain with a pierced heart dangling from it. "Oh, it's exactly what I wanted! Thanks." She scrambled to her feet and gave Charles a hug as Claire let out a happy squeal.

"Look!" Claire stretched a thin gold chain strung with coral beads between her hands. "Oh, super, I can't wait to put it on."

[33]

She rose to her knees on the floor and fumbled with the clasp behind her neck. Marge realized that she was tracing the bare hollow of her own throat with her index finger and hastily folded her hands in her lap. Just like Charles to bring necklaces for the girls. He'd given Marge so many, she'd lost track. Most of them gone now, sold or hocked to get herself through some rough spot or other. She still had the first one, though.

Chuck got a digital watch. "Hey, neat," he said, strapping it on. "But Dad, I'm sorry, I've got a date and I'm late." Chuck winked. "You know how it is, right?" He leered. Marge didn't know whether to laugh or cry. Dear God, what next?

Chuck announced that he had to shave and went into the bathroom and noisily ran water, although Marge had never seen more than a light reddish down on his chin.

"What are you doing these days, Marge?" Charles asked. "Still grinding out term papers for twerps who can't write their own?"

Marge resisted the reply that came to mind. One of the unforgivable things Charles had said, there near the end, was that he'd married her only because she was dope enough to do his work and get him through graduate school. She'd been tempted to send him a bill. Still was, for that matter, whenever the pendulum of "What happened?" began its swing. "I'm still a researcher, yes," she said evenly. "I never do any actual writing."

"Mom's got a super project now," Claire put in, patting the necklace. Marge clamped her jaw. "She's looking up all the unsolved murders in the world for some guy who's gonna write them up in a book."

"That should keep you busy," Charles remarked.

"Not *all* of them, Claire," Marge said.

"And guess what?" Claire continued, as if neither of her parents had spoken. "This afternoon she found a bunch that happened when she was there!"

"Your mother was there?" Charles repeated, his eyebrows rising.

"Some guy tying knots around people's necks," Claire said eagerly. "Crude."

"Really, Claire," Marge protested. Twelve years old, and she reacted to murder as if it were done for her sole entertainment!

"Did you report it to the police?" Charles asked over Claire's head.

"The police!" Marge stared at him while he gazed back with a look of mild inquiry, the foot of his crossed-over leg gently patting at the air. "Why would I report it to the police?"

"Claire said you were there. Don't people who are there usually report crimes to the police?"

"Charles," Marge said, annoyed with herself for letting him annoy her, "I didn't see them. I just happened to be living in the area at the time. I only just realized it, and it all happened years ago."

"Was I there?"

"As close as I was, anyway." Marge clasped her hands a little tighter to keep them from turning into fists. "It was while we were at Oxford," she explained. "A number of young women were strangled after they'd left a pub alone at night."

"I might have heard something about that at the time, come to think of it," Charles said. "I take it this...employer...is interested in British murders?"

The bathroom door banged open, and Chuck came out, his chin a little pinker but not otherwise changed. "Hey, Dad, I gotta run," he said. "Thanks for the watch. It's neat."

"You're welcome," Charles said, one corner of his mouth tucked into a smile. "Now, aren't you glad you stuck around?" He got up and shook his son's hand. They were just about of even height, Marge noticed, startled. Chuck went out and Charles closed the door behind him.

"Tell me more about this job," he said, returning to his spot on the couch.

"I'd really rather not, Charles," Marge said. "It's okay if I treat it like history, but when I really think about it, I get sick. So I'd rather not talk about it."

Charles nodded. "Not the kind of thing I'd expect you to be doing," he said.

"That's for sure."

The telephone rang, and Claire jumped up to answer it. Charles watched her leave the room. "When did Claire get braces on her teeth?" he asked.

"Couple of weeks ago."

"Were they necessary? I never had any. Did you?" He smiled a broad, even-toothed smile, like an indictment.

"Of course they were necessary. Do you think I'm in any position to spend a thousand bucks for kicks?"

"Don't try to guilt-load me, Marge. Who knows what you'd do?"

"You should, for one," Marge snapped. "If you feel guilty, that's your problem, not mine. Mine is to find the money for the braces." She felt rather relieved after this little speech, as if she'd accomplished something.

Whatever it was, Charles took it away. The half grin returned. "You weren't thinking of putting the bite on me, I hope," he drawled.

Peggy snickered.

"I've got better sense than to waste my time. Murder is a little, more profitable these days."

"I changed my life insurance," Charles said solemnly.

"What?"

"I changed my life insurance. You aren't beneficiary anymore. So you wouldn't get anything by killing me," he explained, using the sincere and sensible tone Marge hated.

"Oh, shit!" She jumped up and walked out to the kitchen, where she leaned against the little stub of a counter, grabbing her elbows across her belly. Claire gave her a startled glance and took the telephone around the corner.

Peggy came out into the kitchen and put a hand on Marge's shoulder. "Mom, he didn't mean anything," she said. "Come on back. I've got to go in a couple of minutes."

Marge stalked back to the living room and sat down in the worn-out chair she'd been in a moment before.

"Touchy, aren't we," Charles said.

"How long are you going to be in town, Dad?" Peggy asked.

"Three weeks, this time. I'm on vacation. I'll have plenty of time to be with my family." He looked at Marge and laughed loudly. "Wipe off the sour puss, Marge. I won't be underfoot that much—I've got lots of other friends in this town, remember, and I'll be spending time with them, too."

Women, Marge thought, surprised that she cared.

"Dad, I'm sorry, I'm late for work," Peggy said.

"I'll give you a ride." Charles stood up and fished in his pants pocket for the car keys. "Next week, sometime, huh, Marge? See if you can get these characters to hold still in the same place for ten minutes. I'll give you a call, oh, Monday, and we'll see what works out. I'm tied up this weekend."

"Okay."

"Come on, Peggy. 'Bye, Claire," he called, and opened the door for himself. He and Peggy went out and he slammed the door behind them.

Claire came into the living room. "Where's Dad going?"

"He's driving Peggy to work."

"Is he coming back afterward?"

"He'll give us a call next week."

"Well, how do you like that?" Claire put her hands on her hips and glared at the door. "First he comes barging in with his big *be there*, and then he won't even stay long enough to talk or anything."

Marge flipped her hands helplessly. "What can I do? I try to be reasonable."

"That's okay for you, you're grown up," Claire retorted. She perched on the edge of the couch, where Charles had been sitting, her hands clasped between her knees. "I suppose I have to be reasonable, too?"

Marge said nothing.

"And not cry and carry on or anything?"

"It would be nice."

Claire frowned at her, lower lip lapped over the upper. "Well, I'm telling you, this being reasonable is the pits. It'll kill me someday, see if it doesn't."

"Me, too, honey," Marge said and sighed. "Me, too."

Claire started to cry. When Marge shifted in her chair, Claire got up and ran into her room and slammed the door.

Marge sat back. The lamp beside the couch cast a yellowish light over the cushion Charles and Claire had dented. The cording on the cushion's edge had escaped from its worn casing, and the whole front of the couch was gray with the kind of dirt no amount of vacuuming and shampooing could remove. The

[37]

carpet between couch and coffee table was threadbare. Not what she'd hoped to see in her home at the age of forty-three. Not that any of her life was anything she had expected, back in Oxford.

"Damn you, Charles," she said aloud.

In the bedroom, Claire sobbed.

❊ V ❊

SATURDAY passed slowly, outwardly uneventful.

Marge dragged herself to the library and spent the morning and early afternoon reading about murders that had taken place within fifty miles of where she sat, all in the past five years. A woman who stabbed her ex-boyfriend's fiancée almost a hundred times, then spray-painted her black. A man who, on the advice of his mother, strangled his wife, cut her up in the bathtub, and when the garbage disposal balked, tied up what was left in a couple of plastic sacks and threw them into a nearby lake, all in preference to asking for a divorce. A boy who shot his parents and sister, barricaded himself in their house for two days, firing at passersby, then set fire to the whole sorry mess. And so on and so on.

Marge rode the bus home with more attention to her fellow passengers than usual. She'd found nothing for George Greyborn and was beginning to wonder whether she might not have lost something of her own, some little core of peace and trust in mankind that had always been there to sustain her when she needed it. When she got home, she took a shower four times as long as her usual quick ablution.

One small factor occurred to her, either hopeful or infinitely frightening, depending on which way she turned it: All of these people had struck out at the ones closest to them. They didn't go around doing these things to perfect strangers (although she had read of some who had, she remembered). But then what had set them off? "Nice people," their neighbors testified. "Wouldn't hurt a fly." She remembered those neighbors, from the television news, jowly ladies in flowered dresses standing a safe distance from the "death house," blinking bald men in open-collared golf shirts or suspenders over their undershirts. "Him? (Her?) I don't believe it."

She was clean, although she didn't feel it as she dried herself with one of the soft, ragged-edged towels she'd used so many times. She ran a comb through her hair and pushed the waves into place to dry by themselves, made supper, sat at the table, and talked with her children like a real, live mother. Afterward, hands in the dishwater, she happened to look out the window over the sink and see a squirrel, lit orange by the setting sun, come running toward her across the street. For the briefest moment, she mistook it for a tiny demon.

She read the newspaper, worked the cryptogram, watched the news, went to bed, did not dream.

By Sunday afternoon her cheerful nature reasserted itself, and she had managed to shake off the dirty feeling. It's because of my imagination, Marge told herself. I can visualize too well. If I couldn't make these awful pictures in my head, if the descriptions were only a little more vague, it wouldn't be so bad. And maybe what I imagine is worse than what actually was. A something welling out of a dark I didn't know I had.

"You're awfully quiet today, Mom," Peggy remarked.

"A little tired, is all."

Peggy wandered over to the television, switched it on, watched two minutes of a football game, and switched it off. "I thought maybe it was that date you've got tonight. That you're nervous."

"Maybe I am, a little." Marge sighed. "That's a point. I ought to think about what to wear."

"What about those dark brown cords, and a shirt?"

"Could I borrow your new plaid one?"

"Sure," Peggy said. "If it's clean."

"And my tan pullover," Marge planned abstractedly, staring at the blank TV screen.

"It's funny," Peggy said. "You going out, and me staying home."

"It is, at that." Marge grinned. "Don't worry. I have every intention of behaving myself, and I won't be walking home alone in the dark."

"That's not what I meant." Peggy sat down and half-turned to look out the window, where the deep gold of an elm and the pale yellow of the street maples mingled. "It's just — well — three years ago, when we were still fighting all the time?"

"Mmm?" Marge flinched at the memory.

"I didn't really think of you as being a person apart from us. You know, us kids. You were just a mother. I mean, I knew you

[40]

were a person, of course, but...I'm not saying this very well."

"That's okay." The familiar Peggy faded before Marge's eyes, became a beautiful young woman something like the one who had once inhabited her own mirror. Marge wished life had treated both of those young women a little better. "Go on," she said. "Say it as well as you can."

Peggy turned her head back toward the room, became her well-known daughter once again. "Now, see, now that I'm getting away a lot—going to the U, working, so on—I see it's like we're just a, like a chapter in your life. God, that sounds corny."

"True, though." Marge folded her hands in her lap, noticing suddenly that they were icy. She tucked them into her armpits. Just a chapter, and what would the next one be?

The downstairs door slammed and the windows rattled as footsteps crashed up the staircase. "There's Chuck," Peggy said. "What if I make us some tea?"

"I'd drink some," Marge allowed, smiling again.

"I thought you might," Peggy said. My little girl is growing up, Marge thought. That's corny, too, but it happens. Every mother must have moments like this…. She got up and followed Peg into the kitchen, where Chuck had already buried his head in the refrigerator. No doubt about it, girls were cheaper to feed.

"Something died in here," Chuck announced.

"Too bad it wasn't your appetite." Marge went to look: only the hunk of Port Salut she'd bought in a moment of budgetary recklessness a few days before.

She was ready when Phil came for her. Not just dressed, but ready for the first awkwardness, ready to be apprehensive when they reached the Lindstroms' house.

"Kev and Julie live quite a way from here, other side of the river," Phil said as they went down the stairs. "I forgot to tell you."

"That's okay. I figured it out from the phone number. What's he doing these days?"

"Teaching, still." Phil twisted the key and opened the car door for her. "At the U. I'm surprised you haven't run into him in the library."

"Maybe our schedules don't cross." Marge found the clasp of

the seat belt, buckled it around her while Phil got in. "This is quite the car!"

"It's Pop's," Phil said. "Mine chose yesterday afternoon to throw a brake line. I'd rather drive this one, anyway. It handles so beautifully, it's like it reads your mind."

"So the ads say," Marge said. "What do you drive?"

"Oh, a beat-up old VW bug. More in keeping with my exalted position at St. Podunk's." The engine simply started purring as he turned the key, Marge noticed. Her own last car, a Pinto that had died two winters before, had taken a little more coaxing. Like taking the battery indoors every cold night and reinstalling it in the morning. Hard to do with your fingers crossed inside your mittens.

"I didn't realize writers make enough money to buy BMW's," Marge remarked.

"They do and they don't, mostly don't. Blow the bonuses like a drunken sailor, starve in between, that's the way my old man operates. Always has. That's how come my mother's got a different last name these days. I think this car is the movie rights to a book about a bank robbery." Phil turned cautiously onto a main street. "I can't jockey it the way he does, though. Wrong habits."

"Just don't crack it up."

"Ooo-hoo-hoo! Find some wood and knock on it, quick!"

Marge laughed and gave the side of his head a soft tap with her knuckles. "Is Lindstrom still in English Lit, did you say?" she asked a few minutes later.

"Mmm-hmm. Elizabethans, still."

"Who else will be there besides Marcus Dellingham?"

"I'm not real sure." Phil made a fast left onto a freeway ramp that had Marge trying to put her right foot through the floor. The Pinto would never have held a curve like that. She pulled her foot back, hoping Phil hadn't noticed the reflex.

"There's a bunch of the Oxford-Boston crowd around," Phil continued. "You know how everybody ends up in the same place once in a while. Nothing like a visiting professorship for seeing your old pals, hey? That reminds me, Dick Green might be there. He was at Western Mo when I was. Still the big mystery."

"He caught up with us in Cleveland," Marge said.

"No kidding?" Phil's brief grin was oddly feral in the yellow light of the freeway lamps. "More parallel routes, as you call them. What was the general opinion there?"

"Oh, that he was gay. I don't think so, though. I had a good friend there who was, taught me everything I know about French cooking, and he said not."

"I remember that time he mentioned his high-school girl-friend. Absolute silence fell over three tables around. Were you there?"

"I don't think so. I'd remember that." Marge licked her lips nervously, watching the lane markers glide by. Was she ready to meet all these people again?

"That's right," Phil was saying. "You were never around for the Thursday Tipplers' Club." He maneuvered the BMW past a roaring semi as Marge cringed. "Anyway, this enormous hush came over the whole American crowd, and Dick looks at his watch and says, 'Twenty past,' and everybody cracks up."

"*That* I would remember!" Marge said and laughed. One of their crowd had read somewhere that silences fell upon groups most often at twenty of and twenty after the hour, and for months they had checked the time whenever such a silence fell. "And was it?" she asked.

"Does it matter? Too bad Rosie wasn't there."

Rosie. What on earth was the man's real name? A psychologist with round black-rimmed glasses and a round pink mouth, he had developed the theory that they all unconsciously kept track of the time, and shut up to prove the theory right. Because a lot of the silences had come on time, she remembered.

"Keep an eye out for the Snelling Avenue exit, will you?" Phil asked. "I have this habit of missing exits, especially in this car. She just likes to keep moving." He blended quickly across three lanes of traffic to shift to a different highway. Marge curled her toes to keep from hitting her phantom brake.

"Lindstrom's got some location," Phil remarked as they head-ed south from the freeway some miles later, as calmly as if he hadn't a moment before cut in front of an auto trailer to make the exit. "Two blocks from the humanities building. Can you beat that? When he puts his feet out of bed they're almost be-hind the lectern. Only has to slow down to put on his socks."

Marge loosened her grip on the armrest. "What's his wife doing?"

"Teaching elementary-school art, I think. That's Julie, in case you don't remember." He pulled up in front of a white stucco house, one of the square, forthright houses typical of the area. Marge knew exactly what she would find: past that small front porch with the potted geraniums climbing the steps would be a large living room with stairs going up on the left, a dining room to the right rear, and a kitchen behind the staircase, with doors from dining room and kitchen onto a big, screened back porch. If the oak floors had been sanded and varnished, plain jealousy would put tears in her eyes.

Phil rang the bell.

Under Peggy's plaid shirt, Marge felt sweat break out in little prickles, cool evening or no cool evening. This would really be hard, facing old friends without Charles for the first time. She drew a deep, ragged breath and let it out slowly.

The door opened.

Kevin Lindstrom had put on about fifty pounds since the last time she'd seen him, and his hair was liberally mixed with gray. "Phil, boy, come on in," he said in the same jolly voice she remembered. How odd it sounded coming from this almost-stranger! "And who's this?" He frowned at Marge. "Don't I know you from somewhere?" he asked uncertainly. "You look awfully familiar."

"Kevin, you goose, it's Marge Brock." Julie spoke quietly from somewhere to the side of the door. "How are you, Marge? Nice to see you after all these years. Is this the date you wanted to bring, Phil?"

"It is." Phil sounded pleased with himself.

"Marge, I hope you'll understand, this is a total surprise." Julie turned to Phil, her hands clasped tightly at her chest. "Phil, I wish you'd said."

"Why? What's the matter?"

"It's Charlie. He's coming, too."

"Oh." Phil cast a look of apology at Marge. "Marge, I'm sorry. I didn't even know he was in town."

"It's okay," Marge said. Her voice was firmer than she'd expected. "I saw him last night. I promise I won't make any scenes."

—she lightened the words with a smile—"no matter who he shows up with. It's been six years, after all."

Julie threw her hands apart and gave Marge a light, welcoming hug. She'd aged more gracefully than her husband: still slender, hair still satin-smooth and satin-dark, she looked far younger than her forty-odd years in the slim jeans and pink silk shirt she was wearing. "Come see everyone else," she said, some of the remembered warmth returning to her voice as she evidently decided to make the best of the situation. "You'll know a few of them from the old days."

The floors *had* been refinished. The wall between living and dining rooms had been knocked out, and two thick oriental rugs marked off living and dining areas. And (Marge gritted her teeth and smiled) the Lindstroms had found one of the rare houses with a well-laid fieldstone fireplace, instead of the more common raw red brick. White walls and shelves showed off a collection of folk pottery, a spectacular patchwork quilt hung on the inside wall of the dining area, the kitchen had been completely remodeled: sleek, efficient, food-processored, and microwaved. Marge thought of the elephant of a stove in her apartment and wondered if she could ask the higher rate Mr. Greyborn was paying and still get any decent jobs.

She took another deep breath and plunged into the group on the plant-lined back porch, found a glass of wine thrust into her hand, was greeted and introduced until her head whirled.

"What are you doing these days, Marge?" asked a woman whose name she wasn't quite sure of, a serious-faced woman with her hair drawn tightly into a gray-laced bun. "I haven't seen you since you left for Kansas."

"Charles and I are divorced," she said, "for starters." That wasn't so bad after all, she thought. "I'm hanging on by doing some free-lance research—scuffling through the library stacks and so on."

"Any specialty?"

"Not really." Marge took a sip of the wine. Dry and cold, a pleasure to her tongue. "Right now I'm working for Phil's father."

"Old George Greyborn? Hi, Marge." Marcus Dellingham moved into the conversation shoulder first. "What kind of crime is he exposing now?"

Marge smiled tentatively. "Murder."

"Finally worked up to the big one, did he, Phil?" Dellingham tilted his shaggy head at Marge. "Which grisly goodie is he working on? Our lady of the spray paint?"

"Ick, no."

"Tell him about it, Marge," Phil said. "I'm going to get something to eat. Want anything?"

"Bring me something, I don't care what." The wine was already going to her head, and she'd drunk only half a glass. I'm not used to drinking the way these guys do anymore, she realized.

"Well?" Marcus demanded.

Marge grinned at his eagerness. "He's doing a survey of unsolved murders in the U.S. and Britain over the past fifty years. Well, not a survey, exactly—I guess I'm doing that! A compendium, he calls it, of classic cases."

"Is that the title? *A Compendium of Classic Cases?*"

"It'll never sell," said the woman with the bun. Gwen! It was Gwen! Gwen...? Bishop. Gwen Bishop. Marge wondered where her husband was, the gentle little man with the faraway eyes. Jack, was it?

"I don't know what he's going to call the book," Marge found herself saying. My social instincts seem to be reviving, she observed with mild surprise. "You can bet it'll be snappier than that, though. And I didn't know you were so interested in murder, Marcus."

"Oh, I've made it my hobby," he said lightly. "Found anything interesting?"

"You know," Marge said without thinking, "I did. Did you know there was a string of unsolved murders while we were all at Oxford?"

"The footpath stranglings?" Marcus asked, smiling.

"You *did* know," Marge said. "There goes my something interesting."

"It was all over the papers," Marcus told her. "I don't know how you could have missed it."

Phil handed Marge a paper plate loaded with sliced turkey and little round crackers smeared with shrimp paste and topped with a section of olive. "What, the Oxford murders again?" he asked.

"*I* managed to miss them," Gwen told Marcus. "So, tell."

"Every fourth Tuesday night for about six months, somebody attacked a woman leaving a pub," Marcus said in a lecturer's style. "Right, Marge? So far as the police knew, nobody ever got away, and they never got a good description of the man."

"It *was* a man," Gwen said.

Marc leered. "Unless women have found a way to rape other women and leave the appropriate evidence."

"Oh, Marc." Marge sighed.

"That's all there is to it?" The corners of Gwen's mouth drew down in disappointment.

"Oh, no. Four, was it, Marge? Five?"

"You just said six," Marge pointed out, "but it was seven, as a matter of fact."

Marc raised one eyebrow and an index finger, with which he stabbed the air in time to his words. "Seven women were strangled with a nylon stocking, raped, robbed, and pushed into the bushes beside a footpath. I always thought of the guy as the Footpath Strangler."

"Sounds like a natural chapter head," Phil said, taking Marge's empty wineglass. "I'll have to suggest that nickname to my father. He'll lap it up." He walked away.

"Old Phil never cared for his father's occupation," Marc confided to Gwen. "Something not *quite* about being a crime writer, you know? But I've read every one of the old guy's books. I was really impressed when I found out who Phil was. Talked to the old guy a lot, once, when he was visiting Phil. I didn't know he lived here, though."

Gwen thrust her chin toward him, inviting him to continue.

"I don't think Greyborn ever wrote a book about murder before," Marcus continued thoughtfully, in the same hushed tone. "Mostly he goes for stickups. Banks, armored cars, trains, airplane hijacks. One at a time, in depth."

Gwen looked at Marge. "Why didn't the police just wait for the guy on the footpath, if he was so scheduled about it?" she asked.

Marge opened her mouth, but Marcus answered first. "He used a different place every time. Remember that pub on the towpath, down the river a little? That was one of them. Dead winter, and you remember what the winter of '62 was like over there."

"I used to go shopping just to get warm," Julie said. She offered a tray of sandwiches around. "Where's your glass, Marge?"

"Phil's got it."

"That's all right, then." Julie carried the sandwiches toward another small group.

"I remember taking baths," Gwen said. "Put the electric fire in the bathroom for an hour beforehand, empty the entire so-called hot-water heater into the tub, plus the boiling contents of every pot and kettle we owned, and all just to get warm. Forget clean." She took a step backward, laughing, and brushed at a dracaena leaf that trailed across her hair.

Marge grinned, remembering. "I did the same. Only it didn't always work."

Marcus couldn't be deflected from his main interest quite that easily, it appeared. "Guy killed with his boots on, anyway," he said. "The CID spent a lot of time with its nose to the ground looking for matching footprints in the college quads."

"That lets Charles out," Marge remarked. "He never did remember his boots."

"What's CID?" Gwen asked.

"Uh…" Marc blinked. "I don't remember," he confessed, sounding surprised. "Criminal Investigation Division, I think. Cops, anyway."

"Wait a minute," Marge said. "I thought all of these took place in late '61 and early '62. The bad winter was the next one, wasn't it?"

"You know, you're right," Gwen said with a triumphant-looking glance at Marc.

"You're thinking of the first series," Marcus said with a lift of his chin. "Stopped about the end of April, I think it was. Then nothing all summer, when you'd think our friendly fiend would have been hard at work, and they started up again as soon as classes did in the fall. That should tell you what the cops thought. One word: student."

Phil handed Marge her glass, brim full. She drank half of it down. "I wouldn't know," she said. "We were in Europe all that summer."

[48]

"Long evenings," Gwen said earnestly. "Too much light."

"You might have something there," Marc agreed.

"Marc, you ought to talk to Phil's father," Marge said. "I didn't get nearly that much out of the books I read."

"I can do better than that," Marc said, smirking. "I have all my old newspaper clippings."

"Jesus," Phil said. "What do you want to drag stuff like that around for?"

Marc shrugged. "Why do some people drag five thousand moldering books around half the world?"

"Books are books," Phil said, sounding defensive. "Not a bunch of crumbling newspaper clippings about some dumb murder."

"Is Marc boring you with murder again?" asked a young blond woman, coming up to the group. "Honestly, Marcus."

"Oh, this is my wife, Debra." Marcus took her hand and pulled her into the circle. "Debra, Marge Brock. An old friend from Oxford."

Debra smiled, the sort of smile the mothers of Marge's generation called "engaging," while giving Marge an assessing look. Marge decided Debra had been in kindergarten at the very most in 1962.

"Were you in Cambridge in '64?" she asked Marc.

"Cambridge, Mass., you mean?" Marcus laughed. "I should be so lucky."

"What were you doing?"

"I was a man divided in 1964," he replied. "Worst year of my life. Finished up my doctorate at the University of New Hampshire, living on ketchup and beans, and taught grammar at an academy for wayward girls near Manchester. Hell on earth, that was."

"Is that in Concord?" Marge asked, finishing off her second glass of wine. "The university?"

"Durham," Marc corrected. "Why?"

"Then you wouldn't have been clipping the Boston newspapers."

"No, I don't think I did. Why?"

Marge smiled, anticipating a small sensation. "Oh, there was another series then," she said casually. "I thought maybe you could save me some work."

[49]

"Another series?" Gwen asked. "Of murders?"

Marge nodded. "Just like the ones in Oxford. While a bunch of us were at Harvard. Exact same kind of thing—women walked out of bars and got strangled with a nylon, raped, and robbed. Struck me funny when I read it."

"Weird," Gwen said. "What a ghastly coincidence."

"There's more to it than that," Marge said, accepting her re-filled glass from Phil. "They all had red hair, just like the ones in Oxford."

A little silence followed while Gwen and Marcus blinked at her, punctuated by a burst of laughter from the other end of the porch. One of Kevin's stories, Marge thought.

"Marge, are you sure?" Gwen asked.

Marge nodded, enjoying the attention.

"You're making that up," Marcus declared.

Marge shook her head and dipped her mouth toward the wine. "I'm not making anything up, and I'm sure. I couldn't help but notice, being a redhead myself. It's like being left-handed—you always notice when someone else is."

"Have you told Pop yet?" Phil asked.

"Not yet."

"Maybe you'd better do that tomorrow." Another burst of laughter came from the other end of the porch, and a chorus of groans as a few people realized Kevin had been having them on.

"I'll see him Thursday," Marge said. "That's time enough. Phil, would you get me a glass of water or something before I chug-alug this wine?"

"Go ahead, it'll do you good," Marcus said.

Gwen drifted away. Marge heard her say, "Hey, you know what I just heard?" to the four people making the porch swing creak.

"There must have been a couple of hundred guys in both places," Dellingham mused.

"You don't think they were connected!" Marge exclaimed.

"Marcus thinks everything's connected," Debra said. "That's all he thinks about, is connections." She smiled at her husband, who wasn't paying her any attention at all.

"I mean, it doesn't have to have been any of *us*," he said anxiously.

"Of course not." Marge glanced around and took a canape from a nearby table.

"Nobody in our crowd, I mean."

"Marcus, you're ridiculous," Marge said, her mouth full. She swallowed. "Really."

"It could still just be coincidence," Marc said with an odd intensity Marge couldn't quite account for.

"Could," she said, losing interest. She glanced toward the kitchen, saw Phil turn from the sink with a tumbler of water, and thought about meeting him halfway.

"The party can now begin!" someone announced loudly from the front of the house. Marge stiffened involuntarily, and her heart knocked wildly in her chest.

Charles had arrived.

❧ VI ❧

DEAD silence, into which one voice trailed a couple of words.

"Five to," somebody said. Amazing, Marge thought. They're still doing it, after all these years!

Nobody laughed this time. No one said anything else. This silence was for Charlie and Marge.

He had a girl with him, a willowy blonde with thick maroon eyeshadow and an upswept hairdo that spilled into a crest of sophisticated curls, and who clung to his side with an indefinably childish air.

He looked around the room at the silence, his eyes coming to rest on Marge. He looked surprised. "What in hell are you doing *here?*" he asked.

"I was invited."

"You sure screwed that one up, Julie," he said. "Not your usual form. Where are the drinks?"

"Who is she, Chuck?" the blonde whispered loudly.

"My wife."

The girl, who looked a little older than Peggy, straightened up and took a step away from him, her maroon mouth falling open.

The pounding in Marge's chest eased. "Former wife, he means," she said, smiling kindly at the girl. "Don't let me spoil your evening." That wasn't nearly as bad as I've feared, she thought, fading through the crowd in search of Phil. She met him coming out of the kitchen.

"Here's your water."

"Thanks," she said, taking the glass. "Charles is here."

"So I heard."

Marge turned back toward the porch and found the Dellinghams at her heels. "I wanted to ask you some more about those murders," Marcus said.

"Oh, Marcus," Marge sighed. "Give it a rest, can't you?" She moved away from the kitchen door and found herself next to Charles.

"You could have had the decency to let me know," he said in a rough whisper.

"I didn't know myself until I got here," she said.

"It's damned embarrassing."

Marge gave Charles a cool look. "Your problem." She burrowed her way into the crowd with her glass of water and found herself in the group where Kevin was telling yet another of his long stories. Bored, she backed away. That put her next to the Dellinghams again. Oh, Lord, she thought. Where's Phil?

"What's the matter, Charlie?" she heard Marcus say. "Can't leave your ex-wife alone?"

"Stop it, Marcus," said Debra.

"What's it to you, Dellingham?" Charles said. His voice was almost in her ear. Marge turned.

"Who brought you?" Charles asked her, grabbing her wrist.

"Let go of me, Charles." Marge stared at him steadily. Charles squeezed. The slender leaves of the dracaena brushed over her face as she tried to back away from him. Charles reached out with his free hand and snapped the trunk back.

"Hey," Julie yelled. "My plant!"

"Behave yourself, Charles," Marge said.

"Behave yourself, Charles," he mocked. "What about you, Mommy dear?"

He's drunker than I thought, Marge realized. "Charles, just leave me alone," she pleaded. "There's room for us both."

"At one party?"

Please, God, don't let him break anything else, Marge prayed. Aloud, she said, "Let go of me, please." She was astonished that her voice could sound so calm.

Charles picked her arm up by the wrist and flung it down. Her elbow snapped audibly. A hot pain flooded her arm. She slipped sideways and dashed past him, headed for Phil, rubbing her elbow.

"Who brought you? That's what I want to know," Charles roared, charging after her.

"I did." Phil caught Marge in his left arm, circled her shoulders gently. His right hand still held a glass of wine. "How you doing, Charlie? Long time no see."

[53]

Charles growled and rammed the heel of his hand into Phil's face. The glass splintered on the floor.

Phil danced backward, away from the shards of glass. "Now, just a minute," he began.

The blonde appeared at Charles's side. "Chuck, don't!" she wailed, pulling at his sleeve. "Let's just go someplace else, huh?"

"Shut up, Vikki. I came to see my old friends and I am going to see my old friends," he said. He glared at Marge. "That does not include you, or you either," he said, shifting the glare to Phil.

"Some other time, please, sweetie?" the blonde said.

"Take it easy, Charlie." Kevin Lindstrom's voice was as jolly as ever. "No need to go breaking things. Everybody's welcome."

Charles lunged again at Phil, slipped in the puddle of wine. Phil sidestepped the charge and yanked Marge out of the way. "Let's get out of here," she said. "I don't want to wreck the party."

She scurried backward, into the dining room, as Charles wound up to take another swing at Phil. Phil stepped out of range. "Cool it Charlie, can't you?" he said. He backed after Marge.

She turned, saw Julie standing irresolutely beside the telephone, holding the receiver. "I'm going," she said. Julie nodded and put the phone down. No cops, please, dear heaven, Marge thought. She pushed open the front screen door and ran down the steps, stopped beside the shadowy BMW. A moment later, Phil popped out of the house, and the heavy oak door slammed behind him.

"Let's go," he said, shoving the key into the car door. He gave the key a twist and dashed around the car as Marge flung herself across the front seat and tried to pull up the button on the driver's side. But it was smooth, recessed, no way to get a grip on it. "How?" she shouted.

Phil opened the door with the key, slid into the driver's seat, and started the car, all in one smooth motion. Marge reached for her own door and slammed it as they took off, rounded a corner. "Oh, God," she said. "What got into him?"

"I don't know, but I'm not sticking around to find out." Phil killed the headlights, pulled into a driveway, and turned off the ignition.

"What are you doing?" Marge gasped.

"Get your head down and watch."

A white Buick roared past, screeched around the next corner, accelerated loudly. Marge caught a glimpse of Charles hunched over the wheel as the car went under the streetlight. "He's crazy," she said.

"Could be." Phil started the car and backed out of the driveway, turned on the headlights, and proceeded sedately through a maze of residential streets.

"Oh, no!" Marge exclaimed. "Phil, I left my purse at the Lindstroms'."

He glanced at her, an irritated glance for which she didn't blame him, and made a U-turn. "You wait in the car," he instructed. "I'm going to park a couple of blocks away and go get your purse. Lock up while I'm gone."

"What for?"

"In case Charlie comes back."

"How do I unlock when you come back?" Marge asked.

"Pull up on the door handle."

He pulled over to the curb and got out, leaving the engine running. Marge examined the dash knobs and turned out the headlights. She waited, shoulders drawn together and hands clasped tightly between her knees. What had got into Charles?

The white Buick screeched past, headed back to the Lindstroms' house. If Kevin and Julie never lay eyes on me again, Marge thought, they'll be ecstatic.

Where was Phil?

She closed her eyes, tears of embarrassment slipping down her cheeks. If Charles got there before Phil had found her purse and left... if she had to wait here all night... if Charles got hurt ... if *Phil* got hurt...

A sharp rap on the car window stopped her tumbling thoughts. She saw Phil motion upward, leaned over, and squeezed the door handle.

"This it?" He held out her purse.

"Yes."

He was already in, pulling away from the curb. "He just missed me," he said, panting. "Pulled up as I was leaving. I went over the back fence, got a little lost in people's shrubbery. Jeez, I'm not cut out for this."

[55]

Marge glanced at his heaving chest. "I'm awfully sorry, Phil. I don't know what on earth—why should he act like that? It's been six years, and the whole thing was his idea in the first place!" And just when I was doing so well, she added to herself.

"Second thoughts, maybe." Phil looked over his shoulder. "See who those lights behind us belong to, will you?"

Marge turned around. "It's okay, it's a dark-colored car." She faced forward and began fumbling with the seat belt. "I wonder why he went back."

"You forgot your purse. He forgot the girl."

Marge giggled. After a moment Phil also began to laugh. "It's not even nine-thirty," he said. "What should we do tonight, besides playing cops and robbers?"

"Something without Charles," Marge suggested.

"I'll vote for that. How about going back to my place?" Phil glanced at her. "Play some records, have some coffee. Sober up. I can't take you back to your innocent children with a belly full of wine. Think of the example you'd set."

"There's a lot of turkey in there, too," Marge said with great dignity. "And shrimp."

"Worse yet. What if that son of yours got the idea that shrimp is something to eat? You'd be broke in five minutes."

"True." She leaned back in the seat, suddenly drained and worried. "I don't know when I've been so tired," she murmured.

Phil's hand left the gearshift knob and gave hers a squeeze. "I promise to be on my best behavior," he said. "I grew up in the fifties, too, remember."

"Is that when? Funny, just at the moment I don't feel that young."

Phil snorted. "If what Charlie did tonight is a sample of life at the Brock establishment, I can see why you might feel old before your time."

"You know, that's what's so weird," Marge said. "It's not like him at all—I can remember only a couple of times he ever got mad, maybe three times altogether, except in that last month. The day he left, he was really—well, that's past. Not that we didn't have our problems. Doesn't everyone? But we always got along easily. It all just came apart at once." She was silent a minute or two, remembering. "Boy, was I dumb."

"You seem to have recovered pretty well."

She rolled her head against the back of the seat. "Oh, I'm back together, all right, and the pieces are even in the right places, but it's a bad glue job. A bad glue job."

"I know what you mean." Phil didn't elaborate, and whether he was being understanding or talking about himself, Marge didn't know. He drove cautiously, sedately, across the river on city streets, past the west bank of the university, and into a little warren of streets, where he pulled up in front of a three-story brick apartment house. "Here we are," he announced.

Marge let herself out of the car, and Phil locked her door, then his own. He dealt with more locks on the main door of his building, stopped and picked up a newspaper from the floor of the foyer, and gestured up the stairs. "Second floor," he said. "To the right." As she preceded him up the stairs, he added, "I didn't know you were still seeing Charlie."

"He comes to see the kids when he's in town," Marge explained. "He was over on Friday night for a few minutes. I wonder if he'll have the nerve to call tomorrow. He said he would, but that was before this."

Phil inserted a key into the door of 201. "What about last night?"

"Last night?"

"You told Julie Lindstrom you'd seen him last night."

"Did I? I meant Friday."

The first impression, when Phil turned on the lamp, was of books. Only after that did she see the comfortably cluttered room, with its few good pieces of furniture. Five thousand books was probably an underestimate, she decided, walking toward the shelves.

"Academics," Phil said. "Head straight for the books."

"I'm not an academic anymore," Marge said, smiling.

"Sure you are." He flipped on a light in the kitchenette. "I was serious about that coffee. Want some?"

"Sounds good." Close to the shelves was an invitingly crumple-cushioned wing chair. Marge collapsed into it and stretched her feet out in front of her. From the kitchen came the brief snarl of a coffee grinder.

"You are serious about your coffee," she said.

"Nothing but the best." Water ran into a kettle. Phil came to the doorway, pushing his fist into a coffee filter. "Are you hungry? I have some croissants in the freezer. I can run them through the microwave."

"Not such a purist after all," Marge teased.

"We all have to compromise sometimes," Phil said soberly. He turned away from the door. "Well?"

"Maybe just one." The way to a man's heart, she recalled her grandmother saying, is through his stomach. She wondered idly if the way to this man's heart might not be through her own stomach. He certainly seemed to enjoy feeding her.

She got to her feet and crossed the room to the plank desk under the double front window. "Well, well," she said. "Nothing but the best in typewriters, anyway." She caressed the sleek blue side of the machine. "How long have you had this?"

"The Selectric?" He laughed. "Sorry to disappoint you. It belongs to St. Podunk. I brought it home because I'm writing a paper. It has a Greek character ball."

"Oh, that's right. Classics." She glanced at the Greek-English dictionary lying beside the machine. "Mr. Liddell and Mr. Scott. Haven't seen them in years."

"I bet there're a lot of people you haven't seen in years."

He carried a tray into the room, along with two steaming mugs of coffee and a plate with a half-dozen buttery croissants that presented no appearance of compromise whatsoever, and set it all down on a trunk that served as a coffee table.

"Have some," he gestured. "I'll put on a record. Simon and Garfunkel, okay?"

"Sure." Marge left the desk and sat on one end of the tweedy brown couch, holding the mug of coffee in one hand and resting it lightly on the other. The mug was hand-thrown. It fitted comfortably in her grasp, gave her a feeling of home.

"Do you see many people at all, Marge?" Phil asked. Paul Simon began to sing very softly as Phil picked up the other mug and took the other corner of the couch.

"Not really."

"You've kind of buried yourself in your family, haven't you? Library daytimes, home nights?"

"Something like that," she admitted, tensing. She wondered where he was leading. Not tonight, she thought.

[58]

"What do you do? Read? Novels?"

Marge smiled and shook her head. "A sad thing. I haven't been able to read a serious novel since—well, for six years, now."

Phil grinned. "You can't have despair and experience both," he said. "Novels are too much of an experience. You don't have much social life either, I bet."

"Does it show?" Dear Phil, you are a nice man. I like your looks. I confess a certain curiosity, but I do not want to go to bed with you. Not tonight.

"A little. It's an easy thing to do," he continued. "Burying yourself. You can see, I've done it myself."

Not a room for entertaining, she had to admit. A pleasant room, convenient to live and work in, but meant for living alone.

"I don't quite know how to say this."

She put the mug to her face, sipping, mostly to hide behind the warm brown stoneware, and watched him over the rim. In turn, he stared in the direction of the typewriter, his forehead wrinkled and lips pressed together. He took a deep breath before speaking. Marge found herself breathing deeply with him.

"I don't think you know how vulnerable you are. This job you're doing for my father. I wish, I wish I had never recommended you for it."

Whatever she had expected, that wasn't it. Marge put the cup down and took a croissant. "Why?"

"I—this series of murders you've found. The two of them, taken together. I wish you wouldn't talk about them, like you did tonight. At least not until you've told Pop."

Marge felt her face screw up with puzzlement. "Why not?"

"Can't you see?" Phil said earnestly, shifting toward her and screwing up his own face. "It could be one of us! One of the gang that was at Oxford together, and then at Harvard, I mean. Or even one of the other New England colleges. And if it is, that person is dangerous."

Marge laughed. "I guess so!"

"No, listen. Dangerous to you. You don't know who he is, but does he know that? Pop would know what to do." His lips tightened again and he looked down at his steaming coffee, held loosely on the flat of his crossed knee. "Marge, I'm worried. Something funny is going on. That party didn't feel right, even before Charlie livened things up."

"I didn't notice anything," Marge objected.

Phil shrugged. "Of course, it *could* be my imagination. I'm probably being too sensitive, or something." He took a croissant and began to eat it, looking into space.

"Didn't you hear what Marcus said?" Marge asked. "It could be any of a couple of hundred men, or even just a whopping set of coincidences. They do happen, you know. Or maybe it was somebody who heard or read about the Oxford murders and decided to copy them. After all, how likely is it that one killer was working on both sides of the Atlantic?"

Phil finished off the croissant. "Soggy," he commented, licking his fingers. "You're right, of course, but I've got this feeling. Hunch, whatever you want to call it."

"I call it jumping to conclusions," Marge said, draining her cup.

"More?"

"No, thanks, though it's really good."

"Sure?"

"Well, okay." Phil took her cup and went out to the kitchen. "If you must have it that it was one man," she called after him, "how about a sailor? Working on a freighter, say."

"Oxford's not a port." He handed her a refilled cup and sat down.

"I know that, but it could be somebody's hometown, couldn't it? We think of it as just the university, because the university is so big and so obvious and it was so important to us. But Oxford's a town, too. People live there who never saw the inside of a college. There's that big car factory in Cowley—a lot of people who work there live in Oxford."

"Wouldn't a sailor live in a port?" Phil pointed out.

"It's only a few hours by train from Liverpool," Marge said. "I've made the trip myself. Bristol's even closer. Or London! How could I forget London?" She took another swallow of coffee. "And look at the guy's schedule," she added, hitching forward as she warmed to the theory. "Plenty of time to ship both ways."

"Why would he switch from Oxford to Boston, then?"

"Maybe things got too hot in Oxford."

"Or too cold." Phil grinned. "I did hear that part of Marc's story.

Seems to me they could have caught him by checking whoever turned up looking for treatment for frostbite of the ass."

"We all had that." Marge grinned, too, warm and full of coffee and croissants, and very good ones, too. Ages since she'd had croissants. "What I've got to do is check the dates," she said. "If there's any overlap at all, that lets out all the students, and there goes your pretty theory." She smiled again, feeling brilliant.

"You've had too much wine," Phil stated bluntly. "Almost a year between the last one at Oxford and the first one in Boston, if what you and Marc said tonight is all true. I still wish you'd kept your mouth shut."

"I still think you're jumping to an entirely unjustified conclusion," she said.

"I have good hunches, Marge."

"This one's no winner, I'll tell you that."

He blew an exasperated sigh and sat back against the arm of the couch. Marge sat quietly, thinking about what he'd said. Even if it were somebody in that room—which she didn't for one second believe—she couldn't see how she could be a danger to anyone, not after she'd made the connection in public. It couldn't be silenced, not now. Not if that was all there was to it. Unless the person thought there was something else she might know. Something she might remember, even. She licked her lips. "It's done, now," she said.

"Promise me you'll call Pop tomorrow and tell him about the new series."

"Okay," she said. "I'll feel like a damn fool, but I'll do it. And blame it all on you."

He watched her a moment, his face tense, and then took another croissant. "Have another one before they get cold," he said. "They're no good if you heat them up twice."

She reached for one, broke it in half, put half back.

"Marge."

"Oh, Phil, they're really good, but I couldn't eat a whole one."

"Not that. I'm going to call Pop right now, if it's all right with you."

She glanced at her watch. "It's well past ten. Would he still be up?"

"Pop? If he ever went to bed before midnight, the moon

would fall out of the sky. Hold on." He got up and went into the kitchen. Well, if he didn't feel as silly as he sounded, it was his affair, Marge decided.

"No, the car's fine," she heard him say. "Sitting right here in front of the building." She half listened to the rest of the conversation, half listened to the music while prowling the room. Most of the books were paperbacks, she saw, many of them the kind meant to be bound to match the owner's library, the home-sliced edges of the pages raw and uneven. At eye level, a collection of a dozen or so Hardy Boys novels, the old, good kind. And down in one corner of the wall of shelves, the same group of bright dust jackets she'd seen in his father's office. The older Greyborn's books. She pulled the rightmost one out and looked inside the flyleaf. One every two years, like clockwork.

The record came to an end and she took the needle off.

"I thought you'd want to know, that's all," Phil said, sounding peeved. Pause. "I know the news is on. Oh, all right, go watch it."

He slammed the receiver down and returned to the couch. "Wrong timing," he reported. "Middle of the news. Don't be shocked if he calls you later tonight, though."

"I still think you're making a mountain out of molasses."

"Don't you want the rest of this croissant?"

"No. Listen, Phil, I ought to call home and let the kids know where they can reach me."

"Good idea," he said, eating the other half of Marge's croissant. "You know where the phone is."

It was blue, another little piece of the unexpected that made her look at him again before she dialed. He was just biting off the tip of the last croissant. No wonder he was getting a little pudgy.

Claire answered.

"Claire? Mom. I wanted—"

"Oh, Mom, where are you? I called the other number and they said you'd left! Can't you come home? I'm scared to death! Peggy's not here—"

"Claire, what on earth is the matter?"

"Peg and Chuck decided to go to the dollar movie and it's Daddy, he keeps coming and pounding on the door and I'm all alone—"

[62]

In the background, Marge could hear a muffled thud.

"Oh, there he is again!" Claire wailed.

"I know you're in there, Marge!" Charles shouted, loud enough for her to hear over the phone.

"Listen, honey," Marge said, "I'll be home just as fast as I can make it. The minute I hang up, call the cops, okay?"

"But it's Daddy."

"Claire, he's drunk. Don't let him in, whatever you do. Is the chain up?"

"Uh-huh."

"Then just call the police. The number's right there on the phone. You see it?"

"All right."

"Do it. 'Bye." She hooked the receiver and turned wildly toward the door.

Phil grabbed her shoulders. "What's wrong?"

"It's Charles. He's trying to break into my apartment, and nobody's there but Claire, and she's scared."

"Let's go." He patted his pockets, came up with keys. "Don't forget your purse."

"Right." She snatched up the bag from beside the wing chair and followed him through the doorway.

"I heard you tell her to call the cops. Will she?"

"I don't know," Marge said. "I hope so." She slid into the car and reached across to open the other door.

"Belt up," Phil said. "This silver bullet's gonna travel."

"Okay, Lone Ranger," Marge said shakily. She clutched the seat beside her legs with both hands as Phil rocketed away from the curb.

"Somebody's following us," he said a minute later.

Marge twisted in the seat. "It's a dark-colored car again."

"Same one?"

"I'm not sure."

"I told you there'd be trouble," Phil said, flooring it. The dark car fell behind. A flashing red light followed them for the last three blocks, but they had lost the other car long before that.

The red light ahead of them swung quickly around and around, reflecting off the windows of each house in turn like a passing fire. Marge yanked off her seat belt even before Phil braked behind the stopped police car. She put out a hand to keep herself from sliding into the dashboard, threw the door open, and jumped out, staggering slightly because the car hadn't quite stopped.

"Be careful!" Phil shouted after her.

The curbside door of the police car hung open, and the inside light showed the girl Charles had brought to the party, a policeman leaning close to her shaking head. Marge ran to the open car door. "What's going on?" she asked hoarsely.

"Everything's under control," the policeman said.

"It's his wife," said the girl. Her maroon eyeshadow had been smudged up and over one eyebrow, making her look as though her face had been torn open.

"Ex-wife." Marge's correction was automatic. "Where is he?"

"I don't know," the girl said. "And I hope he stays there."

Marge straightened up and looked up and down the street, but she couldn't spot the white Buick. "I don't see his car," she said.

"He took off about ten minutes ago," the blonde replied. She was trying to light a cigarette without much success, as if it were her first attempt ever. She got it going and dropped the spent match into a maroon silk handbag. "God, lady," she said, drawing hard on the cigarette, "how do you live with a guy like that?"

"I don't."

Marge circled behind the police car, to the street side of the BMW, where Phil was attempting to explain the situation to a patrolman from the second car. "Phil," she said, "I'll be back in a couple of minutes. I'm going upstairs."

She went up the front steps of the house with a nervous glance at the evergreens on each side, remembering Phil's trick of parking out of sight. No one jumped out, but of course the police car was still lighting everything red every couple of seconds. At the top of the inside stairs, another policeman talked through the chained crack of the door, a spill of soft, soothing words.

"Here's my mom," Claire said. The cop turned around.

"What's going on?" Marge asked again.

"Seems like your ex-husband has been trying to get in," the cop said. "You had an argument, I guess?"

"Not really. We both showed up at the same party. I don't know what he was doing—he doesn't behave like this ordinarily." Marge hardly recognized her own tight voice. Why am I making excuses for him? she wondered. I didn't ask for this. "Claire, are you all right?"

"I'm okay." Claire pushed the door shut and Marge heard the rattle of the chain coming off. "I'm sure glad you're home, though," Claire said as she opened the door. "What's Daddy so mad about?"

"I don't know."

"Peg and Chuck aren't home yet. Oh, I was never so scared in my life!" Claire said and gulped. Her face was smudged where she had wiped tears away, and more tears ran over the smudges.

"How'd your face get so dirty?" Marge asked.

"I was hiding under the bed. I was scared he'd break the door down."

Marge put her arms around her daughter. "What should we do now?" she asked the cop.

"I'll come talk to you in a minute. Just let me go tell my partner."

"Oh, no! I forgot, I left Phil trying to explain. Claire, honey, I'll be right back." Marge clattered down the steps behind the cop. "We were speeding, trying to get here fast—"

One of the officers from the second car stood back from the first as she came through the front doorway. The BMW wasn't in sight. A few of the neighbors had come out to stand on their porches, hugging themselves against the chilling night, the yellow rectangles of the open front doorways silhouetting them as their faces flashed red, flashed dark. Marge ran to intercept the man as he returned to his car.

[65]

"What happened to the man I came with?"

"He's parking the car."

"Is it a bad fine?"

The cop looked at her, the light of his own car lighting half his face red, the light of the other alternately lighting the other half. Eerie. Marge stood her ground. "I gave him a warning," the man said. "Since his license was clean, so far. Don't you think you'd better get back and lock your door?"

"Thanks," she said, turning. Phil caught up with her as she ran back up the front walk, and he followed her up to the apartment without a word. The cop who had been talking to Claire came up right behind them. Before Marge could do more than point to the living room, Peggy and Chuck burst through the downstairs doorway and thundered up the stairs.

"What's going on?" Peggy demanded. "There's a police car outside, and some woman in it with makeup like you wouldn't believe, and everybody's standing around looking—"

"You'd better sit down," Marge told her. "It's pretty complicated."

Claire made her report, under the gentle prodding of the policeman. He wrote everything down, promised to check on them on his next couple of rounds, suggested that they get a better lock on the door. "Though he'll either sober up, or get so drunk he can't do anything," the man added. "You'll probably be all right."

"What's going to happen to that girl?" Marge asked. "The one down in your car?"

"We'll see that she gets home."

"Who is she?" Peggy asked.

"She's Dad's date," Marge said. "He showed up at the Lindstroms' party with her."

"He won't bother her too, will he?" Peggy asked. "Go bang her door down?"

"I doubt it," the cop said. "She's just some kid he picked up in a bar. Lock up good, will you?" He pulled the door closed behind himself with a solid-sounding snap. None of the five of them spoke as the man's steps descended the inner stairs and the front door closed behind him.

"Dating you is a considerably different experience than I had expected," Phil observed.

"Oh!" Marge shook her head. "I can't tell you how sorry I am."

"You didn't arrange it, did you?"

"Arrange it! Of course not!"

"Well, then, you don't have to apologize."

Chuck had found half a bowl of popcorn Claire apparently had prepared for herself before Charles had come, and was methodically eating it. Claire glanced at him but seemed to have lost interest in her snack.

"Why didn't you just let him in?" Peggy asked Claire.

"I started to. I even buzzed the downstairs door. But he came up the steps so fast and loud and he was shouting, and I got scared and hid under the bed."

"Why'd you do a dumb thing like that?" Chuck asked through a mouthful of popcorn. "He'd just have dragged you out."

"I—he sounded like—remember? Just before we all moved out, when he said if we didn't he'd kill us all, and he had the carving knife in his hand to cut up the roast, and he tried to follow Mom into the bedroom and she slammed the door, and you and Peggy ran out the back door and I didn't have anywhere to go so I hid under my bed—"

"Oh, honey," Marge said.

"And I guess I just thought it was the same thing all over again." Marge put her arms back around Claire and hugged her tightly.

"He hasn't acted like that since, though," Peggy observed. "Why now?"

"Something must have happened," Chuck said, searching the bottom of the bowl for half-popped kernels.

"Sometimes, when a man gets divorced," Phil said, so softly Marge had to strain to hear him, "it isn't really real to him until he sees his wife out on her own, with her own life going on. And then a kind of loss sets in, a little different than it was before. It gets more real. That could be it."

Who brought you, that's what I'd like to know. Was Phil speaking from experience? Had he raged and carried on the first time he saw his former wife out with someone else? Marge wondered. Somehow, Phil didn't seem the type to have rages. On the other hand, neither did Charles. And she had to be truthful: she'd felt a twinge of anger herself, a twist of jealousy, when she saw the girl with Charles. Marge nodded slowly.

"Would you like me to stay the night?" Phil offered. "In case he comes back?"

"Oh, please," Claire said. "Oh, I wish you would."

"Claire, honey, where would he sleep?" Marge objected.

"He can have my bed." Chuck looked up from the popcorn bowl, a look that said, I'm not big enough to handle this. "I can sleep on the floor."

"I can sleep on the floor myself, for that matter," Phil said. "I think Pop keeps a sleeping bag in the trunk of the car. And since it's past eleven and all of us have things to do in the morning, if I'm not mistaken, maybe we'd better get ourselves sorted out and settle down."

All fine with Marge, except for one thing. As she lay alone on the sofa bed, tensing with each of the occasional headlights that tracked across the ceiling, she wondered what she could possibly feed the man for breakfast.

She woke to the smell of bacon frying.

Sunlight reflected off the windows of the house next door and through the side window into the room, spread into shards of color by the snowflake prism Marge had hung from a thread thumbtacked to the top of the upper sash. She could hear the quiet voices of her family in the kitchen. The bed felt warm, safe. She closed her eyes.

She hadn't bought bacon in six months.

But she did smell bacon. An old song her father used to sing, a cowboy song, he said, started going through her head. *Wake up, Jacob*, something, something, *bacon in the pan, coffee in the pot, come along and get it while it's hot.*

Phil must have gone out while I was asleep and bought bacon, Marge thought. What time is it, anyway? The kids have to be in school by quarter to eight!

"Mom?" Chuck asked from the doorway. "Phil wants to know, would you rather have your eggs in an omelet, or sunny side up?"

Eggs! "An omelet sounds good," Marge said. "I'll be along in a minute." She rolled over to look at the clock. Ten past seven already. She swung her feet to the floor and put on her old corduroy robe, shivering for a moment in the chilly fall air.

In the kitchen, remains of four breakfasts littered the table. "I thought you should sleep if you could," Phil said apologetically. "Peggy said you'd want to get up." He did something at the stove. Eggs shrieked as they hit hot butter. "Don't worry about the mess," he said over the *ship-ship-ship* of the fork. "This was all my idea, and I'll clean up."

"I'm not worried about cleaning up. Eggs, Phil? Bacon? Where did they come from?"

"The supermarket over on Park is open twenty-four hours," he reminded her. "I ran over this morning, as soon as I had inspected your refrigerator. Do you really have oatmeal every morning?"

"Pretty nearly," Marge admitted. "Oh, my goodness. Sausage, too?"

"Ah, so I got carried away." Phil set the omelet, delicately browned and creamy where it had cracked slightly, in front of her with a flourish., "*Voilà*," he said, grinning.

"Lovely. Almost a shame to put a fork into it," she said, putting a fork into it. "Tastes good, too." She pointed the fork first at Claire and then at Chuck. "You and you have to get going. Now."

"You don't have to nag," Claire sniffed. "I am a responsible human being." Mmm, Marge thought. We're at that stage already, are we?

Peggy got up and began stacking dishes in the sink. "I said I'd get those," Phil objected.

"You didn't say I couldn't help."

Phil shrugged. He'd tied one of the flour-sack dish towels around his waist. Marge looked down at her plate with a muffled smile. The towel rose to follow the gentle outward curve where his T-shirt met his belt. He really did look funny, domestic. Dear.

"Bye, Mom," Chuck called. "We're going."

"Have a nice day," Marge replied.

"Mom?" Chuck had stopped at the door. "You will be all right, won't you?"

Marge took a deep breath, unwilling to be reminded of the

night before. "I'll be fine," she called. The door closed behind Chuck and Claire, and Peggy went soft-footed down the hall to put the chain up.

"I guess we'll hear from Mr. Mandelbaum," she said when she returned.

"Who's that?"

"The landlord," Marge said, sighing. "Because of last night, Peggy means. The old lady in the front apartment downstairs has a complaint for anything at all. So far, we've escaped."

"Only by living like mice," Peggy said.

"She had a fit when we moved in," Marge recalled. "Took one look at Chuck—this was four years ago, mind you—and decided any boy that age came with an electric guitar."

"We'd have been lucky to buy him a kazoo, then," Peggy said.

Or now, Marge thought, but didn't say. "So she wanted it in the lease that the kids couldn't have musical instruments. But Mandelbaum's sister owns a music store, so he wouldn't do it. Very entertaining for a while."

"Mrs. Nemesis—her name is really Miss Finster, but we call her Mrs. Nemesis—threatened to move out. So he told her go ahead, her rent was only that low because of rent control," Peggy continued gleefully. "So she came up and asked what we were paying, and Mom told her it was none of her business, so she decided that it had to be real low because Mom was divorced and probably *available*—"

"With three kids in the house," Marge murmured, not looking at Phil and wondering if the heat in her ears really meant she was blushing.

"So Mrs. Nemesis went to Mandelbaum and demanded the same rent Mom was paying, and he said fine and raised hers seventy bucks."

"Peggy, Phil doesn't want to hear about all this."

Phil's mild hazel eyes looked amused. "Actually, I find it very interesting," he said.

Peggy shrugged. "That's all there is, really."

"And is the rent low?"

Outrageous question, Marge thought.

"Three-fifty," Peggy informed him cheerfully.

"Low," Phil agreed.

Peggy grinned. "Why do you think I'm living at home, instead of at the U?"

Marge pushed herself away from the table. "I think I'll go get dressed," she said. "The library opens at nine, and I do have a job."

In the bathroom, she pulled her nightgown over her head and examined herself in the mirror. Not as she was at twenty, but not too bad, she decided. A touch angular. She put on underwear and a sweater, listening to the clink and splash of dishes in the kitchen, and as she climbed into her jeans heard Peggy tell Phil about the fuss Mrs. Nemesis had made over the man in the back downstairs apartment. He and his girl had argued; she'd slammed his door and run out, leaving the house door wide open. "*Anybody* could have come in," Mrs. Nemesis screeched, "and murdered them in their beds!" Marge smiled as she padded back to the living room for her socks and shoes. Peggy told a funny story.

But the guy's lease hadn't been renewed.

Phil drove Peggy to her nine-o'clock class and doubled back to the library with Marge. "Those must be strong genes of yours," he remarked. "To produce three redheads."

"Not really." Marge watched the traffic ahead. It was beginning to thin out a little now. "Charles's mother was a redhead, too."

"Oh, really?"

Marge shook her head with a rueful smile. "What a creature she was! She had really bright red hair, not at all like mine. In fact, the first time I ever met her she told me I had such a nice, tame color of hair, just the shade of a cockroach."

Phil gave her a sharp glance. "You've got to be kidding. She said that?"

"Watch out!"

"Sorry." Phil swerved to miss the motorcycle braking in front of them.

"Yes," Marge said, answering his question. "I wish I'd had the wit to ask her how she knew what color a cockroach is, but I was only nineteen. What can you expect? She was something, all right."

"Was," Phil repeated. "She's dead, then?"

"Yes. She died just after the beginning of our second year at Oxford. Charles flew home for the funeral."

A few minutes later, Phil slipped the little car into the bus stop in front of the library. "Be careful," he said, leaning across the car to look up at Marge as she got out. "If Charlie makes more trouble, call the cops. Or call me. Or both. Or if anything else.... I wish you'd get in touch with Pop and talk to him about these two series, okay?"

"I'll give him a call later. I've only had a day and a half on the Americans, and that one case is really the only good one I've come across. I'd hate to waste his time." Marge glanced up as a large red bus threatened to nudge the BMW out of the way.

Phil seemed quite unperturbed by the monster behind him. "You won't be wasting his time," he assured her. "He'll be as excited as a Doberman with his teeth in a T-bone."

"He wasn't last night," Marge said, but Phil had already pulled his head back. The car scooted into the stream of traffic, and the bus huffed up to the curb. Marge watched the BMW dart around the next corner, and slowly climbed the library steps. Her own life was complicated enough without this job interfering. But she was stuck with it now. Stuck, or curious? she wondered as she hauled open one of the bronze doors. How much poking around in her old friends' lives could she do without offending anyone? Just to rule them all out, of course. She didn't for a minute believe any of them would go out and do murder—not this kind of murder, anyway. She'd love to see Phil's face when she could say, "I told you so!"

Phil has to be imagining things, she told herself as she let the microfilm catalog whine toward the M's. Viewed in the cold light of day, it was all so very long ago! How could anyone feel threatened now, after getting away with it all these years?

Careful, Marge, she told herself. You're sounding more like Phil every second. She copied down another dozen catalog numbers, most of them for books on the open shelves, and wearily headed for the stacks.

✷VIII✷

MARGE closed the book she had been reading with a thump, stretched, and glanced at her watch. Three-thirty. The elderly man at the other end of the table was looking at her with a faintly worried air. She smiled briefly at him to show that she wasn't about to explode into some kind of unreasonable behavior, like muttering to herself or eating a loud apple, and opened the last book in the pile. The carmine and black jacket boded ill as far as gory pictures went, as did the numerous gray streaks along the edges of the pages, so she held her trusty index card ready as she began to read.

The prose style was something by Shakespeare out of the *National Enquirer:* difficult to sort facts from fury. But she kept at it, because the book was a good one by Greyborn standards. The chapter notes were long and specific, and the cases discussed were all fairly new and sometimes unsolved. As were, for example, the ones in Kansas in 1966 and 1967.

Déjà vu. The feeling that one has been through all this before. Marge drew a long breath through pinched nostrils, her heart knocking softly at her throat. This author favored her with a photograph of one of the stockings, mercifully removed from the victim and placed on a neutral background for the camera. It could have belonged to anyone at all. No, not just anyone, she discovered by reading the caption. Tests run on the sweat deposited by the wearer had revealed a type O. The victim's blood was type B. Proof that the stocking had been carried to the site by the killer and hadn't been taken from the victim. And why should it have been? Nobody wears stockings and jeans, not in August. Not in Kansas.

Marge felt an odd cool wave pass over her body.

This author wasn't interested in hair color. Marge made a note to Mr. Greyborn to check it. Three victims, this time, spread over seven months: the Footpath Strangler—he'd have to be renamed, Marge supposed—was slowing down. If, by some incredible chance, it was the same man.

"Are you all right, young lady?"

Marge looked up at the elderly man. He had come to her end of the table and was bending over her with the same worried air she had noticed before. "I'm fine," she said.

"You went quite pale."

Marge put her hands to her cheeks. What do I say? she wondered. That I'm letting Phil's imagination run away with me? "I read something a little upsetting."

The man gave a satisfied nod. "Forgive my asking, but you aren't in any, er, difficulty, are you?"

Startled, Marge examined the lined, fine-boned face. He looked guileless enough. "Not really."

"I don't like to interfere in others' business as a rule, but I must say I am glad you have returned," he said, a little above a whisper. "I couldn't help noticing this morning that after you arrived, a man came in behaving in a most peculiar fashion."

"Oh?"

"Yes." The elderly man nodded solemnly. "He peeped in at the door, most cautiously, then circled behind the magazine racks, glancing at you the while as if to be sure you could not see him. Then he sat down with a magazine all the while you were reading with that, er, card." There was a hint of a question in that last sentence, to which Marge didn't respond. "When you got up to go, he followed a moment later," the man continued on one long, sighing breath. "Leaving the magazine for others to put away, I might add."

Must have been when I went back to the stacks, Marge thought. She glanced swiftly across the room, saw no one she recognized. "Is he here now?"

"No. He didn't return when you did."

"What did he look like?"

"Quite ordinary, I must admit. Somewhat tall, perhaps, although I find height difficult to judge when sitting down. Brown hair."

"What color eyes?"

"That, I'm afraid I can't tell you." The man smiled sadly. "I can't make out much detail at that distance anymore, and I was wearing the wrong glasses. All I could tell was that whenever I looked up from my reading, he seemed to be looking at you."

Marge felt her shoulder blades draw together. "Thank you," she half whispered. "I'll be on the lookout."

"I do hope he isn't following you for any, er, nefarious purpose."

"Me too," Marge agreed, flashing a quick smile. "I wish I knew who it was. But I know a lot of men who fit your description." She stared past the elderly man's shoulder, feeling her face begin to tense. Charles, perhaps? Up to some unimaginable new trick? "Thanks for telling me," she said, smiling again. "My name is Marge Brock, by the way."

"How do you do." He took her offered hand with fingers as cold as her own. "John Whitney. Pleased to be of any service to you. I do hope I'm mistaken about that man."

"Maybe he's lost interest."

"One would hope." John Whitney returned to his usual seat with a gracious nod.

Marge looked back down at the book and tried again to reconstruct life in Kansas fifteen years before. Peggy had been a preschooler, Chuck an infant. Except that Marge had had a miscarriage just before Thanksgiving that first year, Kansas hadn't been much different from any other new place. Impossible to differentiate one bit of academia from another. She remembered chiefly the shock of that sky, so open above her head after the grayer, closer horizon of the Northeast that she felt as if her brain had been exposed, trembling, to its light.

And she certainly didn't remember any murders.

Giving up, she marked her place in the book, put it into her briefcase, and left the reading room.

The bus stop was breezy and cold, and so empty that she knew she had missed a bus by only a couple of minutes at most. She peered down the street and saw none coming. What would Phil say about this latest batch of murders, if the second one had put him in such a swivet? she wondered. She smiled, imagining his mouth falling open.

The third batch would at least have the effect of eliminating some people, if they really were three interconnected series, she reflected. After a moment or two, she left the bus stop in front of the library and walked five blocks to the downtown B. Dalton's, where she expended six dollars and tax on a Rand McNally road guide. She could think, offhand, of at least three people she could check up on. Right after dinner, she'd get at it. With any luck, she'd put them all out of the picture and put Phil's hunch to rest for good.

"Can I borrow your compass, Chuck?" Marge asked.

"If I can find it." Chuck unwound his feet and left the living room with a backward glance at the football game. "Tell me if anybody does anything great."

Marge was saved from having to pay attention by a time-out and a car commercial. Three minutes later, Chuck came back and handed her the compass. "What's that?" he asked. "Are you planning a trip?"

"No. Just looking up some distances." She opened the guide to Kansas and located the three towns in which the 1966 murders had happened: Olathe, Overland Park, Shawnee. Setting the compass for an arbitrary thirty-five miles, she drew a circle around each town. All three circles included the city of Lawrence.

Her scalp prickled.

Wait a minute, Marge, she told herself. Wait just a corn-huskin' minute. Every one of those towns is closer to Kansas City than to Lawrence. And just where is Western Missouri College?

She searched the map for a few minutes, then thought of a better way and went into the girls' room. "Claire, is the dictionary in here?" she asked.

"Don't tell me there's a word you don't know!" Claire rummaged under her bed and came up with Marge's old *Collegiate*, a tired volume held together with black electrical tape. A much younger Marge had written in next to the colleges listed in the back the names of those in her high-school class who had gone to each of them. She resisted the temptation to look at them all and turned to the end of the list. Western Missouri College was in Kansas City, Missouri.

Not quite so far west, she remembered. But they thought it was.

Not quite so far west, but still within range. Nobody thought twice about driving thirty miles, not out in Kansas, not in 1966.

She went back to the book with the red and black jacket that she'd checked out that day. No information about the victims' hometowns. Whether they'd been robbed, the author didn't say.

Two more questions for Mr. Greyborn. Marge added them to the hair-color question on the index card she'd started that afternoon. Who are you kidding? she demanded silently. It's you who's playing detective, dummy. Go back to the cryptogram.

Which she did, for the whole three minutes it took her to work out WHITE CHRYSANTHEMUMS SUPPORT WILD CHRYSALIS. A cheer from the crowd on the television made her look up. She gazed blankly at a man in a light-colored shirt jumping up and down in a circle of teammates. Dick Green, that was the other one at Western Mo, besides Phil.

Phil?

She shook her head violently and picked up the road guide again, turned to the New Hampshire page. Manchester was a little over fifty miles from Durham, according to the chart at the top of the page. So Marcus must have had a car. At first she hunted for Durham directly north of Manchester, but found it at last in the southeastern corner of the state. About seventy road miles from Boston, it looked like.

Not so far. Not so terribly far. And Manchester was even closer by a different route.

Marcus?

Where had he been during the Kansas murders? (Assuming that they had some similarity to the others besides the stocking, she reminded herself.) Marge squinted at the TV without really seeing it. Surely the Boston papers made it into New Hampshire! Why had Marcus been so insistent that she'd been making the story up?

"Y-e-a-y!" Chuck cheered. Somebody had kicked the extra point, and his team was ahead.

Marc's hair could be called brown, especially by someone used to the barley-white hair of the local Scandinavian-descent population, although Marge herself always thought of it as a dark blond. And Dick Green's hair was brown, beyond question. Both men were also on the tall side of average.

Marge got up and went into the kitchen and dialed Mr. Greyborn's office. He wouldn't be there, of course, but he might have an answering machine.

No such luck. And his home number wasn't in the book. She looked up Phil's number and dialed that, but he wasn't in.

"What's the matter, Mom?" Chuck asked.

[77]

"I'm trying to figure something out," she said. "I wish Peg were home." To tell me what a jackass I'm being.

"She's at the library, I think." Chuck's words came out muffled. How did he manage to get food in his mouth without my noticing? Marge wondered. I must really be preoccupied!

Julie Lindstrom.

The idea unfolded itself in quiet, complete beauty, almost with the faint rustling of a peacock's tail. Smiling to herself, Marge found the Lindstroms' number and dialed.

"Hi, Julie," she said. "Marge Brock. I wanted to apologize for last night. I hope the party wasn't ruined?" True enough, she thought, listening to Julie's disclaimers, but that's not all I want. She poised her pencil above one of the index cards and crossed mental fingers for Julie to be in a talkative mood. "I really don't know what got into Charlie," she said. "He's never acted like that before. If I'd had any idea—"

Julie made soothing noises.

"I'd really hoped I could spend some time, you know, catching up with everybody," Marge said.

Half an hour later, she sat down on the couch and contemplated her delicately extracted list of names. Almost impossible to believe, even knowing the academic tendency to travel in cohorts.

There was Dick Green at Western Mo with Phil. And Marcus Dellingham had been "in some hick town in Kansas. We used to see him once in a while when we were in St. Joseph," according to Julie. That meant eastern Kansas, most likely, and her road atlas showed St. Joseph linked to Kansas City by fifty-odd miles of highway. So Marcus couldn't be eliminated. Not back then, before fifty-five started saving lives.

She smiled briefly at that, then sobered. She couldn't cross off Kevin Lindstrom, either. Not if she allowed Marcus. Once again, she stared unseeing at the television, remembering Pallas Athena Lindstrom sitting on her father's lap in the pub on Iffley Road while Julie took her turn at billiards. Not possible. But none of them was possible. And what a long time ago all of it was! Why bother about it now?

"How much longer is that game going to last?" she asked.

"Dunno. They've almost finished the third quarter."

She glanced at her watch. Five of ten. "What if we switch to another channel long enough to watch the news?"

"Oh, Mom," Chuck said, groaning.

"The thing goes on forever, Chuck. I want to get some sleep tonight, and you need to, too. Just let me see the first twenty minutes or so. Then you can switch back after the weather. I don't care about sports."

"Tell me something I don't know." Chuck flipped the dial and clumped out to the kitchen. Marge followed, to try for Phil and his father one more time before the news came on. No luck.

Say, a couple of hundred men who could have been at Oxford, then Boston two years later. Then narrow it down some more. But how much more? Would a dozen be reasonable? When she knew of five, herself? "I wish I knew something about statistics," Marge complained, leaning against the refrigerator door. "Or about migratory patterns, or academic populations, or whatever."

"If you don't even know what you want to know, I don't know how you're going to know you know it when you do know," Chuck observed.

"Don't eat all the peanut butter," Marge said. She levered herself away from the refrigerator door, which opened before she reached the hall. "Can I fry up some of this sausage?" Chuck called after her.

"Unless you want it for breakfast."

The news had come on while she was out of the room, after all. On the screen as she walked in was a picture of a plump, pretty girl with wavy short hair. "And in a tragic note," the anchorman read, "the body of Sandra Jane Foster was discovered near a path in the Wood Lake Nature Reserve early this morning, by a man walking his dog."

"Dogs aren't allowed in the nature reserve," Marge objected illogically as her knees collapsed her onto the couch. The scene shifted to a wrapped-up shape being lifted into an ambulance.

"Miss Foster had been strangled with a nylon stocking, according to reliable sources," the anchorman continued as the ambulance sped away from the camera. "She was last seen alive in Goody Sam's, a bar on West Lake Street, in the company of a tall, brown-haired white man. Miss Foster was wearing dark slacks and a white, long-sleeved shirt. She is described as five feet, six inches tall, about one hundred forty-five pounds, and had blue eyes and auburn hair." The anchorman stared solemnly out of the screen.

Marge rubbed her face, as if she could rub away her disbelief.

"Police are asking that anyone with information on Miss Foster's whereabouts later Saturday evening call them." A number, almost illegible in black and white, appeared at the bottom of the screen.

"No," Marge said. "No, no, no."

"On the national front…"

"Are they done with the weather yet?" Chuck asked. "Hey, Mom, what's the matter? Are we having a nuclear war?"

"Oh," Marge said, almost a sob. "Not that bad. But bad enough. A girl got killed, the way the girls I've been reading about got killed."

"Girls get killed all the time," Chuck shrugged.

"Oh, I know, I know," Marge said, sitting up straight on the couch.

"You worried about Peg?"

"Peg!" A chill slowly formed in Margie's stomach. "Yes, I guess I should worry about Peg."

"Oh, Mom, she'll be okay."

What was it Peggy had said? Just the other day. Karate lessons. A good idea.

The telephone rang.

Marge got up to answer it and was greeted in the hall by a cloud of greasy smoke. "Chuck, the sausage is burning!" she yelled, snatching up receiver and pan lid at the same time and trying to say hello and smother the fire, both at once.

"Hi, Margie. It's Phil."

"Phil! I've been trying to get you all evening. Put some baking soda on that, Chuck."

"What's wrong?" Phil asked.

"I found another series. In Kansas. And—oh, Phil!" She stopped, forced a yawn to open her throat. "There's been one here," she cried.

"Killing?"

"Yes," she said, her voice back under control. "On the news just now. A redhead, strangled with a stocking."

"Where's Peggy?"

"She should be in any minute. She was at the library," Marge said.

"Marge, do you want me to come over?"

Phil's voice was soft, concerned. Marge closed her eyes and leaned against the door jamb. "Please," she said.

"Be right there."

Marge hung up. Was that a wise thing to do? she wondered. Have him come here? Suspicion! She let her head sag into her hands.

"Was that Phil?" Chuck asked.

Marge nodded. "He's coming over."

Fortunately for her heart, beating so hard she could see the pulse flutter the front of her shirt, Peggy came up the stairs just a few minutes before Phil. The three of them talked so late that Phil just sacked out on the floor again.

❦ IX ❦

For the second morning in a row, Marge awoke to the mouth-watering aroma of good food. This time it was the yeasty odor of a freshly baked coffee cake.

No denying it. A man like Phil Greyborn was very easy on the taste buds. She squeezed her eyes closed and turned over, pulling the covers tightly around her shoulders.

The telephone interrupted her thoughts. Someone picked up the receiver after the first ring. Reluctantly, Marge unwound from the blankets and reached for the corduroy robe. Phil was talking in a low voice; she couldn't make out any of his words. Nine o'clock! She stared at the clock, but the second hand was moving: it must be right. What could they all be thinking of, letting her sleep so late?

She hurried into the bathroom with her jeans and shirt rolled around her underwear and hustled into them. As she walked into the kitchen, Phil was just pouring out a cup of coffee.

"Sleep well?" He pushed the cup toward her. "I hope you like almonds. This coffee ring is full of them." He smiled, a shy little smile.

"Phil, why do you keep feeding us like this? It's wonderful, but—"

"You look like you need it," he said, putting a thick slice of the coffee cake on a plate and setting it in front of her. He looked older than he had last week, Marge noticed with a pang of conscience, more lined and sagging. None of us has the resiliency we used to have, she thought, unconsciously smoothing her cheeks upward with her fingertips. She sat down and picked up the piece of cake, bit into it. Delicious. "What was the phone?" she asked.

"Pop wants to see you, but first he has to catch a little sleep, and then he has some other things he has to catch up on, so he'll be running around all afternoon. So he wants to know if you would mind going over to his office this evening."

"I guess," she said unenthusiastically. "If there's a bus that late."

Phil thoughtfully cut himself another slice of the almond ring. "I've got a seminar to teach, but I can give you a ride over if you want. If you can stand the VW. Pop wants his car back by this afternoon."

"Thanks, I'd like a ride. Where is everybody?"

"Claire and Chuck went to school, and Peggy is working an early shift. She said she'd be back around two."

"I'll be at the library."

"Marge." Phil sat down opposite her and folded his arms on the table. "I wish you'd give up this job. I know you need the money, but I'm afraid for you."

Marge regarded him steadily for several seconds. Her first thought was to tell him how silly his theory sounded, but then she remembered the little list she had so painstakingly put together the night before. "*For* me?" she asked, in spite of what would be danger if the whole charade were true. "Or *of* me?"

He blinked. "What's that supposed to mean?"

"All these murders!" Marge exclaimed. "You know about the Boston ones, the Oxford ones. And I told you about the ones in Kansas last night—three, near Kansas City, in 1966 and 1967."

Phil licked some icing from his fingers.

"The book didn't say if they were redheads, but everything else fits. They even showed a picture of the stocking from one of them."

"And?"

"Five of you were there in 1961. Close enough in 1964. Close enough again in 1966."

He thought that over for a minute or two while he cut himself a very thin slice of the coffee ring. "Does that mean I'm one of your five?"

She couldn't quite say yes. In daylight, with sunlight just sneaking into the kitchen, the idea was doubly ridiculous.

"Damn it, Marge, I'm trying to keep you away from whoever it was! I'm looking out for you!"

"I know that, Phil, but—"

"How could you even think such a thing?"

"Damn it, Phil! How do I know who to trust? After everything that's happened to me?" She pushed her plate away and turned her head.

"Calm down, Marge. I wouldn't ever hurt you, please believe me. Now, don't you see that you have to tell my father to get somebody else to work for him on this? None of the old crowd will know who it is, so it'll be safe for the new person, and I can spread the word that you've quit."

"No."

"Marge, please."

"I can't quit now. Don't you see that? I have to *prove* it couldn't be any of you, otherwise I'm always going to be wondering...." She pressed her lips together and stared at him. One tear slid down her left cheek.

"And if it is one of us? Your five?"

"Then I have to know who."

He sucked at his lips, the way his father did when he was thinking. "Why not just go tell the cops?"

She shrugged and got up to get a tissue.

"All of it. The Oxford murders, the ones in Boston. The ones in Kansas."

Nose buried in the tissue, Marge nodded again.

He tilted his head as if to say, be reasonable. "Why not let them find out? That's their job. They're even pretty good at it, if you can believe Pop. If there's something to dig out, let them dig it out."

"And what will I know?" she asked, her voice muffled by the tissue she still pressed to her nose.

"They'll catch the guy. Then you'll know."

Marge reached for the coffee cup and drained it. The coffee was cold and bitter. "Three separate police forces have let him slip past them already," she pointed out stubbornly. "And now I'm going to work."

Phil sighed. "Okay, okay. I'll give you a ride. I've got to go home and change anyway, and Pop's ready to report the damn car stolen." He untied the dish towel from around his waist and patted his pockets. "Will you give the cops your list of names?"

"No."

"Why the hell not?"

"Don't snap at me, mister. This whole nonsense was your idea, and they're your friends, too." Marge clattered down the stairs, pulling her jacket on, leaving Phil to close the door.

"You'll need your briefcase," he said, handing it to her as he caught up beside the car. She took it without thanks. In the BMW she sat with her jaw forward and said nothing. After a time, Phil began whistling through his teeth.

The tune stayed in her head all morning, infuriatingly familiar as she gritted her teeth and took notes for his father. Finally, words began to come through: *She's my little deuce coupe....*

Beach Boys, for Pete's sake. Marge put her head in her hands.

"It's all right, Mrs. Brock," said John Whitney from the other end of the table. "He's not here today."

"Thanks, Mr. Whitney," Marge said. "I needed a little good news."

The day clouded slowly as she worked, leaving the reading room in a gloom only partly relieved by the fluorescent lights someone turned on around noon. Sometime in early afternoon she began looking at the pictures in the book she was reading, no matter what they showed, with a calm acceptance that frightened her. Twice, she half got to her feet to call Mr. Greyborn and tell him she couldn't come that evening, and twice, although it was Tuesday and she knew Miss Turki would be in the office to take the message, she sat back down.

By the time she ran for the bus shelter, it was raining, long tear shapes against the acrylic walls that made it hard to read the numbers on the buses, so that she almost took a 6B instead of a 68. And by the time she had walked home from the bus stop at the other end of her ride, she was soaked through.

"Any mail?" she asked Peggy.

"Couple of letters. No bills."

"I'm going to get out of these wet clothes, then."

Marge changed, taking her time, and picked up the letters Peggy had left on the kitchen table. "Oh-oh, a missive from Mandelbaum," she said. "About guess what." She tore open the envelope and scanned the landlord's hope that the untoward events of Sunday night would not be repeated. "You and me both," she said, then looked at the other envelope.

[85]

What could Charles want? She remembered suddenly that he hadn't called the night before, not that she could blame him. The note came out of the envelope wrapped around some bills. Ten twenties, to be precise.

"Two hundred dollars!" Marge exclaimed. "In cash, through the mail! Oh, Charles, you idiot!"

"What's the note?" Peggy asked.

She skimmed it quickly. "Dear Margie," it said.

> I want you to know I'm sorry about Saturday night.

"He must mean Sunday," she murmured.

> I'd been drinking and I've been under a terrific strain. I guess I should tell you this is no vacation I'm on. I got laid off. Well, fired if you have to know the truth like you always do. Same old thing, nobody understands. I came up to try to work up some old contacts and see what I can find. There's nothing for me in St. Pete, the bastards won't even give me a reference.
>
> The enclosed will help with Claire's teeth. Don't worry about the amount, I'm okay for cash for a while yet. Call you later this week.
>
> Charles

"Well?" Peggy asked.

"Money for Claire's teeth. He's lost his job." Marge tossed the note onto the table. "Read it yourself if you want."

Peggy left the note where it was. "Mom, you look bushed," she said. "Why don't you go lie down for a while?"

"Thanks, I think I will." Chuck had the couch occupied, watching *Scooby Doo*, of all things, so she went into his room and flopped on the unmade bed. The rain spattered on the window beside her head, turning the room gray.

She sagged almost immediately into a light, troubled sleep. Flashes of memories went through her head as if they were dreams: Charles pushing Peggy in her stroller down the streets of Cambridge, sunlight on his smiling face. Marge's mother telling her severely that if she had to go through with the divorce, she had to do it without help: It would build her character. Claire as a baby, shrieking with delight as Charles played peekaboo. A familiar face glimpsed in the lobby of a movie theater, a face she had thought was hundreds of miles away. A ghastly drink called rum-and-baby something that Tony Owens used to drink.

She came awake and stared at the grayed-over ceiling, wondering if life would ever make any sense again.

"Mom?" Peggy stood in the doorway. "Was there something in particular you had planned for dinner?"

Marge thought for a moment. This job had even dislocated her usual careful meal planning, she thought resentfully. "Eggs, I guess," she said.

Peggy didn't move. "There's an awful lot of stuff in the refrigerator," she said. "Maybe you'd better come have a look."

Marge put her feet on the floor and stretched, feeling as if every joint of her body needed a lube job, and went into the kitchen, blinking against the light.

"Like these." Peggy handed her a package of meat. "I don't even remember what they taste like. Do you know how to cook them?"

Marge looked. Lamb chops. Eight of them with little pink paper panties on. "Good grief," she said. "What are we going to do with that man?"

Peggy grinned. "Let him feed us, don't you think?"

"Phil," said Marge an hour later, "I appreciate the lamb chops, but I wish you'd stop feeding us."

Phil gunned the little yellow VW away from the stop sign at the end of the block. "Yeah, I got carried away again. But I hate to see wide-open spaces in a refrigerator—too many of them when I was a kid, I guess. Don't you even get food stamps, Marge?"

"Not under the new rules. Not with Peggy working, too."

"But she's spending her money on college!"

Marge laughed. "Income is income, Phil. Don't you know that?"

"What if you didn't report it all?"

She shook her head. "I've been tempted. But they know I can work, so I'd just have to go back to somebody's typing pool. Better this way."

"Bureaucracy," he snorted. He reached toward the dash, and the windshield wipers doubled their speed.

"It's not the end of the world," Marge said. "I can always sell a pint of blood if I get stuck. They never turn a universal donor down."

"That's horrible." Phil gave her a quick glance and slowed down. "You don't really mean that?"

"Sure," she said cheerfully.

"Horrible," he repeated. The wind unloaded some rain from the trees they were passing under; it thumped on the roof of the car with a dull rataplan. Phil cleared his throat a couple of times. "I never was much good at saying things, Marge."

"Shush."

"I just hope we get out of this mess. Soon. I have other things I want to pay attention to." Other things. Not me, Marge thought. "I wish you'd—"

"—quit the job," Marge finished. "No, I won't. I bet your father won't, either."

"Oh, lord, no." Phil looked as if he ought to have a cloud over his head labeled "Gloom," like a character in a comic strip. "Fat chance of that!"

"You know, you can't even be sure it is a mess," Marge said. "It's still all your hunch."

"I have good hunches," he told her again.

I'm glad I never told him Mr. Whitney's story, Marge reflected. He'd have me in protective custody, or something. She looked out through the rain-flecked window. The day had darkened early: the lights of the storefronts they passed as they crossed a main street reflected yellow and red in the drops of water. And it was getting chilly. Marge snuggled into her raincoat.

"Cold? I can put the heater on."

"No, thanks."

She liked this city. When they'd moved here, in 1972, it had been almost like a homecoming, very different from their other moves. She hadn't been pregnant, for one thing, she thought with a smile. And always before, there had been other stresses:

England, for all the language similarity, was undeniably a foreign country. Coming back, after three years there, was nearly as strange—the cars too big and the money too small, and something in herself, or maybe even something in America, changed. And then Kansas! Cleveland!

But here, she'd felt almost instantly comfortable, happy with the small-town friendliness of her neighbors, thrilled with the big-city life. With a rare glow of contentment, Marge watched the faces of the houses, the lighted rooms, glide by under the old trees.

Phil flipped his turn signal on, recalling her to the present. Almost there.

"Phil?" Suddenly panicked. "Did you see a white Buick parked back there?"

"On the side street? Relax. Different model."

"Are you sure? It looked just the same."

"Marge, be sensible. What would Charlie be doing over here?" He started to angle toward the curb, stopped. "You want me to go around the block again so you can make sure?"

"No, that's okay. You're probably right." But what if it had been Charles in the library? What if he had followed her to that last conference? Then he'd know where Greyborn's office was. Charles might be waiting, ready to intercept her!

Cool it, Marge me lass, she told herself. The logical place for Charles to intercept you is at home. And what difference would it make if he did know where Greyborn's office is?

What if he wanted to raise a scene, without the kids hanging around? He couldn't do it in the library...

She half turned to Phil, lips parted to tell him about the man in the library. No. He'd never leave her alone to work. Calm down, lummox. The man wasn't there today. And what do you know about Mr. Whitney, besides "shhh"?

Phil opened the car door for her and they climbed the steps of the old house together. Marge was surprised to see a light in the window of Bellflower Press and both young men gesticulating at one another. As Phil pushed the front door open, it became obvious that another editorial conference was in progress.

"Anytime we get a folder decorated with flowers, I can tell you two things," one of the young men bellowed, his beard jerking in time to the forefinger he pounded on his other palm. "It's crap, and you'll want to print it."

"Well, hotshot, let me tell you something..."

Whatever it was, Marge didn't hear. Phil closed the door of his father's office behind them, reducing the shout to a distant yammer. Mr. Greyborn called to them from the inner room.

"Pop, I'm warning you," Phil said without even a hello. "I'm doing my damndest to talk Marge into giving up this job. It's just too dangerous."

George Greyborn tilted his chair back and made a peak of his fingers. "Phil, you're turning into a class-A worrywart in your middle age," he said. "Pay no attention to him, Mrs. Brock. He always has gone off half cocked."

"Pop!"

"Not only that, you've lost whatever sense of adventure you used to have. Comes of teaching at St. Podunk's, I don't doubt. Find some chances to take! Spice up your life!"

"Oh, hell. Have it any way you want." Phil turned and opened the outer door. A scrap of poetic argument floated in. "But at least put her in a cab to go home, okay? So she doesn't have to walk to the bus?"

"It's not even really dark yet," the older man pointed out. "And I don't propose to keep her here all night." •

Phil made an inarticulate sound and went out, closing the door behind him considerably more firmly than necessary. "He thought up better exit lines than that thirty years ago," his father observed. "Don't pay too much attention to him. He's upset with himself."

"Himself?"

"Don't you see? He's attracted to you, but he doesn't know how to tell you. Old sweaty hands all over again."

"Oh," Marge said, a little taken aback by this turn of the conversation.

"He'll probably feed you, if you let him. Like his mother, that way. When words fail, bring on the soup."

Marge chuckled. "I did find some lamb chops in my refrigerator this afternoon."

"Lamb chops!" The elder Greyborn laughed. "Great merciful heaven, I had no idea he was that serious! I'd watch out if I were you. Now, shall we get down to business? I see you've got quite a full folder there."

Makes efficient use of time, Marge thought, echoing one of the evaluation slips from Peggy's elementary school. She gave Greyborn a mental check mark. "You think all these cases are really connected, then?" she asked.

"The Oxford and Boston ones, certainly." Greyborn nodded. "Altogether too similar not to be connected. If not the same man, then one who was familiar with the Oxford murders and deliberately copied them. About the Kansas series, I'm less sure. I'd have to know more details before I'd count that."

"And the Foster girl? Does she fit?"

He shrugged. "She does seem to, doesn't she?"

Marge nodded. As an exercise in probability, she'd have to agree. "Is that all you wanted from me?" she asked. "Because it's still not very late, and the rain's slacked off. I can take the bus home."

"Suit yourself." Greyborn scribbled some more notes to himself. "See you Thursday afternoon, right?"

Marge nodded and motioned him back to his seat as he started to rise with her. "I can find my own way out," she said.

From the office of Bellflower Press, a sullen silence spilled into the hall, an almost visible miasma spreading from the two young men. She wondered if she should say good night, but neither of them as much as glanced her way, so she went straight out. She paused on the front porch, looking down the neatly laid brick walk. It was darker than she had thought from inside, and for a moment she considered going back and asking Mr. Greyborn to call a cab after all.

But the streetlight reflected from the wet bricks encouraged her. Once she got past the plantings near the house, everything would be clear, and it was only a couple of blocks to the bus stop. She started down the steps.

The swish of the junipers warned her.

Her own disbelief canceled the warning. A hand clamped over her mouth and dragged her off her feet. She tried to bite, then to scream. All that came out was a strangled sound that scared her even more. She raised the heavy briefcase to batter at the legs behind her, but the swinging weight wrenched her wrist, and the briefcase flew into the shrubbery. The man shifted his grip, off-balance. She got her feet under her, tried to hook a foot behind his knee. No good. Go for his feet. Stamp. He hugged her head to his wet chest, the hand still over her mouth and tasting metallic.

She stamped again, cursing the silly style that had her wearing soft joggers instead of the spike heels of twenty years before, tried to jump, landed on a foot.

A groan of pain. The man let go. She screamed.

Bellflower Press erupted from the front door, and her attacker fled. The lead young man fell flat on his face on the brick path, and the other one clumsily jumped over him and gave chase. Marge ran after him, hoping to glimpse the man who had grabbed her. He was, she saw with glee, running with a limp. But the streetlight showed only a ski mask, an anonymous gray sweat shirt, anybody jeans. Bellflower Press, also in jeans and gray sweat shirt, slowed, stopped, returned.

"Sorry," he said thickly as he passed her on the walk. "Too much Triple Sec."

He went up the brick walk, exuding an aroma of orange, and trudged up the steps. His partner sat on the porch rubbing his knees. George Greyborn stood in the open doorway.

Somewhere not far away, a car started.

"Did you get a look at him?" Greyborn asked excitedly. "Did you see who it was?"

Marge shook her head. "He was wearing a ski mask. But I stomped his foot pretty good. He was limping."

"Good for you," Greyborn said, applauding. "I guess I'd better give you a ride home after all, though."

So once again she settled into the front seat of the BMW. On the way toward the main street, they passed the white Buick, still parked where she had seen it. It was, just as Phil had said, a different model.

"SHOULD we have called the police, do you think?"

George Greyborn glanced at Marge sideways as he drove, much the way his son did.

Greyborn drove in silence for several minutes. The rain began again, heavier than before, a real October rain. "Looking at it objectively," he said at last, "yes, we should have called them. We can do it from your apartment, if you like."

Marge considered the option. A reluctance to bring this elegant man into her rather shabby apartment decided her. "Let's give it a miss," she said. "They probably couldn't do anything, anyway. As long as I'm out of it without any damage, I'm ready to forget it."

"Without damage," Greyborn repeated in a ruminative tone. "I wonder if that might not mean something."

Marge chuckled. "It means I can stomp like an angry rhinoceros when properly motivated," she said, exhilarated by the memory of the man's painful-looking run. "Too bad Bellflower Press was so drunk. I'd like to have ripped that ski mask off."

"It might have settled a number of things." Greyborn's voice was remote, oddly expressionless. Marge sneaked a quick look at his profile, as remote and expressionless as his voice.

"Will you tell Phil?" she asked.

"Not unless you want me to." The tires stopped hissing on the pavement as the car slowed to turn into Marge's street.

"Good." Her ebullient mood returned. "He'd only nag me to give up the chase. Now that things are happening, though, I think we may find out a few things."

She was aware of Greyborn's head shaking. "Don't do anything foolish," he said. "Don't tempt fate."

"It isn't a question of tempting fate," she said. "But I bet Phil was right. I bet the murderer was at that party the other night, or else heard of it, and now he's taking action. It's new to him, and he's sure to give himself away."

"Are you sure it's new to him?" Greyborn's voice seemed to recede into an even greater distance.

"You think it isn't?"

"Look in my right-hand coat pocket."

Marge put her hand into his coat pocket and felt something damp wadded up there, something soft and familiar-feeling. She pulled it out and held it up to the faint light from the windshield.

Greyborn stopped the car and put on the inside light. Marge was looking at a leg cut from a pair of pantyhose. She stared at Greyborn, her glee fizzling. "Where did this come from?" she whispered.

"I found it on the sidewalk while helping my young friend to his feet."

"You're joking." Marge tried to remember the path: the young man sprawled on the bricks, the gleam along the edges of the bricks in the yellow light of the streetlamp. She couldn't get an image of the stocking, but there had been many shadows.

"I assure you, I'm not joking." Greyborn turned his eyes toward her. She had the feeling he wasn't seeing her at all. "I'm beginning to think Phil might be right, Mrs. Brock. Perhaps we should give you a break for a few days. If it's not already too late."

"Too late?" Nothing around the car but shadow, the thick, clotted shadow of the maples that had been so welcome in the long summer days.

"It could be that you are now a threat simply because you know these murders have been done," Greyborn said. "Something you may not know about, consciously, may be ticking away in your memory, ready to explode at any moment. And that time bomb is dangerous to the murderer. Or he may simply believe that to be the case, which comes to the same thing. Either way, he may want to, shall we say, defuse the bomb."

Marge looked at the stocking in her hands. She balled it up and thrust it deep into Greyborn's pocket, wiped her palms down the fronts of her thighs.

"I'll call you, Mrs. Brock. We'll work out some equitable arrangement as far as pay goes. Now I suggest you go straight upstairs and lock your door."

Marge looked out and saw that they were parked in front of

her house. She gave Greyborn a subdued thanks and did exactly as he had suggested.

It wasn't even eight o'clock, she saw when she got in. She checked on Claire and Chuck, decided to work off her nerves by scrubbing the kitchen. The mindless motions did prove soothing, although they did nothing to help her accept the idea that her game had suddenly turned deadly. At least her heart stopped pounding. She was contemplating the otherwise almost unthinkable step of cleaning the oven when the telephone rang.

"Hello, Marge. How'd it go with the old man?"

"Hi, Phil." She hesitated. "Not bad."

"He have any new ideas?"

"Not really," she said. Phil sneezed. "Bless you."

"Thanks. I think I'm getting a cold," he said, as if he weren't really thinking about it. "I'd stay in for a couple of days if I didn't have to teach a ten-o'clock class tomorrow."

"That's too bad." Keep the conversation on neutral ground, she told herself. Don't cry on the phone. "How'd your seminar go?"

"My what?"

"The seminar you taught this evening," she reminded him. Haven't I had this conversation before? she wondered.

"Oh! The seminar. Fine." He sneezed again.

"Bless you," Marge said. "Take care of that cold."

"You are all right, aren't you, Marge?" he asked in a rush. "No trouble getting home or anything?"

"No, none at all. Your father drove me, as a matter of fact." She picked at a chunk of something dried onto the kitchen table. Not as thorough as I thought I was, she decided.

"That car is going to know its way to your house all by itself if we're not careful," he said.

"Phil, what's the matter? You sound funny."

"It's this cold coming on."

"No, it's not." She was suddenly quite positive. "You're fishing for something. What's up?"

"I just wanted to be sure you were okay." He sounded hurt.

"I already told you, I'm fine." She narrowed her eyes, put one and one together, and got seven. "You haven't been talking to your father, have you?"

"Well…"

"What did he tell you?"

"He said there was a little problem." Phil sneezed again, twice.

"Phil, I'm fine. I don't know what your father told you, but discount it 100 percent. Take care of that cold, will you?" she added warmly. "Want me to come over and fix you some chicken soup?"

"No!" She heard a sharp breath. "Absolutely not. You stay put. But thanks," he said, his voice softening. "Glad you're okay. Good night."

"Good night." Marge hung up, feeling both amused and dissatisfied. It would be nicer to have him here, she thought. Wearing his silly dish towel. Already she was ready to wake to coffee perked and breakfast on the table.

Not tomorrow, though. She went into the living room to roust Chuck away from the television and get ready for bed. Her right heel was a little tender, another reason for wearing something stiffer than joggers when struggling with ski-masked men.

Damn Greyborn, though. He must have gone straight to Phil and told him all about it.

The alarm woke her from the sort of stunned sleep that follows long hours of circling, sleepless thought. She perked her own coffee: two days of Phil's idea of breakfast had been quite sufficient to break her of her frugal cup of tea. What will I do when this is over, she wondered, and I have to go back to the old budget?

"Mom?" Peggy called. "Can I borrow a pair of pantyhose?"

"Sure. Just look in my top drawer, will you?" Marge called back. She stirred the oatmeal into the boiling water and put the lid on the pot, turned the flame down. No omelet, no almond ring. Damn the man.

"I could have sworn I had another pair," Peggy said, coming into the kitchen. "Not there now, though."

Marge turned out the flame under the oatmeal. "When did you have them last?" she asked, the automatic phrase a mother uses to greet a child's announcement of a loss.

"Oh, I don't know. You know how it is with hose."

Troubled, Marge tried not to think what she knew was about

to come into her head—that maybe Greyborn hadn't gone straight to Phil. That Phil had been, to all intents, alone in the house while she was asleep, for probably an hour yesterday morning.

That she'd never actually spoken to his father about going to see him: Phil had arranged it.

That it was Phil who tried so hard to make her quit this job.

That the dropped stocking had been cut from a pair of pantyhose. A neutral color. Could be anybody's.

Like all the others.

"Peggy," she said, surprised at the steadiness of her voice, "do you have one of those maps of the university handy?"

"Yeah, sure. Want it right away?"

"If you don't mind." Marge set out the bowls and spoons, poured herself a cup of coffee and one for Peggy, checked the oatmeal. "Claire!" she called. "Chuck! Breakfast's ready!"

"Here you go," Peggy said.

Marge took the class bulletin and set it on the counter while she dished up the oatmeal. "Breakfast!" she called again.

"Okay!" Claire yelled.

Marge picked up the class bulletin and thumbed through to the map of the campus. St. Anne's was completely surrounded by the university, just as Phil had said: It was that funny Gothic building she'd wondered about from time to time on her way to use the university library. A parking lot to the east of it was marked, St. Anne's. The south-facing windows at the end of the upper stacks of the library might overlook that lot, Marge calculated.

"Do you have a nine-o'clock class this morning?" she asked Peggy.

"Yeah, but I'm going straight to McDonald's afterward," Peg said. "For the noon rush."

Marge set the oatmeal pot in the sink and ran water into the pot. "Chuck! Claire!" she shouted again.

"I'm shaving!" Chuck shouted back.

"What for?" Claire asked from the hall. "Just to tie up the bathroom?"

"I'll ride over to the U with you," Marge said to Peggy. "There's something I want from the library."

[97]

"I'm getting a little spoiled for the bus these days," Peggy said, sitting down. "I sure could get the automobile habit in a hurry."

"Mmm."

"Something the matter, Mom?"

"Not really," Marge lied. She sat down herself and looked at the oatmeal, which looked placidly back. Somehow the dull emptiness she felt didn't seem much like hunger, but she ate the oatmeal anyway.

Peggy chattered happily through the bus ride. Marge tried to keep up, to look bright when brightness seemed appropriate, to answer in more than one syllable. The effort seemed to work: They parted on the steps of the library with a cheery wave from Peg. Marge took a deep breath and walked down to the entrance plaza of the building. Please, God, she heard herself whisper. Please, let me be wrong. She didn't even stop to check the bulletin board to see if her research service ad was still posted.

Five minutes later she had found a window from which she could see the St. Anne's parking lot, with its neat identifying sign in cutesy Gothic letters. The main entrance of the St. Anne's building faced the library, something she hadn't realized from the map. Nor had she realized how close it actually was: Marge was glad of the library's sleek windows, bronzed glass that reflected the outside world away.

She had to go to the bathroom.

But it was too late to leave now. If she did, a man coming to teach a ten-o'clock class might well park his car and be inside the building before she got back.

Her legs were getting prickly from standing still. Someone else was in the stacks close by: she could hear the slide of books in and out of the shelves, soft footsteps.

A yellow Volkswagen appeared at the far end of the St. Anne's parking lot and came slowly toward her. It ducked into a space in the middle row. Stopped. Nothing happened for an interminable time, perhaps ten or twelve seconds. The door opened, sagged shut, opened again.

Phil got out of the car and closed the door. He paused. Locking the door, Marge told herself. He walked away from the car, a gawky gait no different from what she had watched a few days before, but she couldn't see his legs; they were hidden by the other cars.

And then he came out onto the fifteen feet of sidewalk that led to the main entrance of St. Anne's, and yes, he was limping, and yes, it was the right foot.

Marge rubbed her palms together, where her nails had dug little crescents into them, and turned away from the window. She walked down the stacks at a moderate pace, found the ladies' room, waited for an empty cubicle.

Rather surprised, she lost her oatmeal.

Again at a moderate pace, she crossed the campus to the bus stop, waited twenty minutes for the bus. Got on the bus. Paid sixty cents. Rode. Got off the bus. Walked the few blocks to her house, past the yard where white alyssum still frothed under its lacy blanket of birch leaves, past a small boy on a tricycle who said hello, past the corner house with its golden chrysanthemums leaning on a weathered split-rail fence, up to her own front door. Climbed the stairs. Found the other key. Let herself into the empty apartment. Lay down on the couch, face down.

And only then began to cry.

❄XI❄

THE city, in the throes of assorted budget cutbacks, had threatened to close the police station closest to Marge's apartment so
many times that she was somewhat surprised to find the station
still there. She got a second surprise when she pushed open
the heavy glass doors and climbed the four inside steps: What
faced her was a virtual duplicate of the dull green office in
Chuck's (and before his, Peggy's) high school. Instead of the
faded woman with the harlequin-frame glasses, there was a
sad-eyed man with a paunch, who heard her story and referred
her to a trim young black woman in uniform. The policewoman
supplied her with a cup of burned-tasting coffee and took her
into a back room in which there were four items: two chairs, a
table, and a typewriter bolted to the table.

There Marge repeated and amplified the story she'd told to
the man with the paunch, answered a number of questions,
and sat quietly with her hands folded on the purse in her lap
while the younger woman fed a form into the typewriter and
clacked away for a couple of minutes.

"Why didn't you report this last night, Mrs. Brock?" the woman asked suddenly, turning away from the machine.

Marge shifted her hands on the purse. "I told you. It didn't
really seem that serious, somehow. I wasn't hurt, and I got a
ride home."

"No damage done, in other words." The officer shook her
head, her full lower lip tight with what was perhaps disgust,
and made a note on a spiral pad in rapid shorthand. Marge tried
to read it upside down. The first word seemed to be "complain-
ant."

"But then I got to thinking," Marge continued when the shorthand had stopped and a silence had stretched for several seconds. "Maybe I'd better say something in case…that girl the
other day…"

The officer nodded. "Why do you think Mr. Greyborn failed
to report this attack?"

"Maybe he thought it wasn't too serious, either. Or that it was too late to do anything, anyway," Marge said with a quick, humorless smile to take the edge off the words. The policewoman responded with an identical smile of her own.

"You make our job harder when you delay," she said.

"I know that." Marge let her fingers twist together. "I'm sorry."

"You think you may have injured this assailant?"

"He was limping when he ran away." Her head and shoulder twitched of themselves, as if to say, pay no attention to that.

The policewoman turned back to her typewriter. Her strong brown fingers rattled a few more words onto the form she had started to fill out, while Marge looked from corner to corner of the cream-colored ceiling. Unlike the ceiling corners of her own apartment, they showed no evidence of having been visited by spiders. The room had one narrow window, on which a dark green shade hung a little crookedly and which had a sturdy metal grille on the outside. Depressing.

"You want to read this over and sign it, Mrs. Brock?" the officer asked. "This here is all your vital information," she explained, pointing out the name, address, age, and other irrelevancies Marge had given her. "Then this is a summary of the complaint."

The summary took three sentences. It's a summary of a summary, if you only knew it, Marge thought as she signed. She left the police station and walked slowly to the end of the block, where she perched on the edge of a bench whose back advertised a family restaurant, to wait for the bus.

Some corner of you doesn't believe what you saw, Margaret Rosten Brock, she said to herself. Some corner of you has rejected that stocking completely, or you would have told that nice policewoman about it. And just why is that? Because you don't rat on a man who buys you lamb chops?

A bus lumbered down the street and ground to a stop. Marge hurried up the steps before its cloud of oily exhaust could catch up with it. She dropped some change into the fare box and slumped onto one of the side-facing front seats to continue her ruminations.

If you had to report it to the police at all, why didn't you do a complete job of it? she asked herself again.

Her hand came up to cup her cheek as she remembered her face against the man's—Phil's—wet chest. No wonder he's catching cold, she thought. Poor guy was probably standing out there in the rain for almost an hour, waiting for me to come out.

Because he didn't really try to hurt me, she thought. And because he called to be sure I was okay. Her right ankle flexed and slowly extended a little guiltily as she thought of stamping on his foot. But then, what about the stocking? Had he meant to use it? Or what?

"It doesn't make any sense!" she exclaimed aloud.

"Nothing on earth makes sense, lady," the bus driver responded. "Best thing is just to go with the flow." Marge bit her lips, embarrassed.

The buildings of the university began to appear to the left of the bus, across from Marge's seat. She found herself stretching to see if she could spot the St. Anne's parking lot, but it was too well concealed in the center of the university. She had no hope of spotting a little yellow car.

And why should I want to? she asked herself, angry.

"University library," the bus driver called out. A pair of girls in sweaters and plaid skirts got off the bus. Marge felt incomplete, as if she were leaving something terribly important undone just by keeping her seat. Habit, she supposed. Two years of getting off the bus at one library or another, out of plain necessity.

"Marge! Hi!"

"Fare, mister?" the driver yelled.

Marcus Dellingham backed up and dropped some coins into the fare box. "Hi, Marc," Marge said without much spirit.

"Hey, what a piece of luck! Just the girl I wanted to see." He plopped down in the seat beside her, eager as a puppy. "In fact, I was going to call you tonight. You headed anywhere in particular?"

"Just going home."

"I'm taking a late lunch. Can I buy you one? At Jimmy's. You know the place?"

Something twisted in Marge's chest. "Yeah, I've been there."

"Greatest roast beef sandwich in the world," Marcus bubbled. "Really. Come on, say you'll come with me, even just for a beer. I want to talk about your murders."

"They aren't my murders!"

"Oh, cool it, you know what I mean. I found all those old clippings, if George Greyborn wants them."

"Clippings?" Marge blinked at the storefronts going past on the other side of the bus. "Oh, those. Marcus, I'm sorry, I completely forgot about them. It's been a weird couple of days."

"Oh." Marcus shrugged away the flat syllable. "You don't have any notes with you," he said.

"I'm not working on that job anymore," Marge told him. "I'm between jobs, I guess you'd say."

"Then you need lunch," Marcus exclaimed, apparently delighted. "Great, that's settled. You'd have to get off almost in front of Jimmy's to transfer, anyway, so come on."

Marge smiled slightly. "Okay, I'll let you buy me a lunch, just to keep you happy," she agreed. How does he know I have to transfer? she wondered, feeling suspicion begin to move again, like a mental fetus. She pinched the bridge of her nose.

"Headache?"

"Just tired, is all."

They had left the university far behind, and the bus was now headed down a seedy-looking avenue beside which an occasional maple tree struggled to survive. A strange neighborhood, really, of pre-1900 houses ranging from burned-out, boarded-up shells through rooms-to-let with old men sitting on their steps, to newly renovated family homes, slate roofs repaired and bright new coats of paint over the narrow clapboard siding.

"Deb and I are thinking of buying around here," Marcus commented.

"Who's buying houses these days?"

"You can get one for back taxes," Marcus said. "You have to contract with the city to fix it up in a certain amount of time, but it's a real good deal."

"Fixing up takes money."

"We've got a little," Marcus said. "Enough to get a start and hope something turns up."

The bus pulled up in front of a Seven-Eleven store with iron grilles over its windows. "It's a high-crime neighborhood, Marcus," Marge remarked. "Ought to suit you right down to the ground."

"It's gonna get better," Marcus began, then realized she had been joking and laughed. "You know what's funny? I used to want to be a crime reporter. Then I discovered I can't stand the sight of blood."

"That would be a handicap," Marge agreed.

"Never occurred to me to do something like old George Greyborn does—best of both worlds, that. Even after I talked to him so much when he was visiting Phil, while he was researching that book on the attempted theft of the crown jewels, I didn't have it figured out. I can be awfully dumb sometimes."

"Marcus, you're crazy," Marge diagnosed.

"Yup," he agreed comfortably. "Only way to go. Hey, here's our stop."

At two in the afternoon, Jimmy's was almost empty. Marcus chose a table near the bar and raised his hand at the waitress lounging against the polished surface. She said something to the bartender and came toward them. "Want to try the roast beef?" Marcus asked Marge. "Or, no, you said you know the place. What do you want?"

"Roast beef is fine with me."

"They say the pastrami's good too. I hate the stuff, myself," Marcus said with an exaggerated shudder.

Something was missing from Jimmy's today. After a moment, Marge realized that the jukebox wasn't playing. Her heart must have been pounding; she felt it slowing down. "Roast beef sounds good," she repeated.

Marcus lit a cigarette and kept up a steady stream of light conversation while they ordered and waited for their lunch. When the sandwiches came, he sobered, giving Marge the impression of a newscaster shifting from a humorous story to a serious one. "Marge, I've been thinking about what you said the other night," he announced, frowning. "A lot."

"I try not to, myself," she said.

"I've got about a zillion questions for you," he went on, as if she hadn't said anything. "I wish I'd caught you while you still had access to your notes. I suppose Greyborn's got them all?"

Marge nodded. No point in telling him the shorthand notes were still at home. He'd only want her to transcribe them. The roast beef *was* good, as good as the pastrami. Be careful, lady, she told herself. You get used to eating this well now, you're in real trouble.

"Damn shame," Marcus said. He stubbed out the cigarette and took an enormous bite out of his sandwich. "I don't suppose you can remember any references," he added, chewing.

"They're all in the catalog at the public library. They must have a hundred books about murder."

"You didn't read them all, did you?" Marcus exclaimed. His eyebrows disappeared under his mop of sandy hair.

"I at least skimmed most of them."

"Oh." Marcus took a deep breath and sighed heavily. "More of a job than I thought. I wish I could get a look at your notes."

Marge tilted her head and considered. "If you come out with a book before Greyborn does, he'll have little green-eyed kittens," she said. "He's already got a contract and a deadline."

"Book! I don't want to write any book. Too much like work. I've got enough trouble perishing, without publishing." Marcus finished off his sandwich and hooked a napkin out of the table dispenser. " 'Nother one?" he asked, signaling the waitress.

"No, thanks. One's plenty." I must be skinnier than I thought, Marge told herself. Everybody keeps trying to feed me.

"Well, I'll just have to pump you," Marcus said. "You've got time, haven't you? With no job? I've got all afternoon." He laughed. "Don't look so dismayed, Marge. You'll have me thinking I'm unattractive, or something."

"How on earth would I manage that?" Marge asked, but Marcus bubbled on.

"I reread all those Oxford clippings," he said. "You know, our guy went in a different direction every time. And you know something else? I got out my old bus map—"

Marge's mouth sagged open. "Marcus, how do you ever move? You must keep everything that ever comes into your house!"

"Not garbage," he said seriously. "Anyway, listen to me, will you? This guy, every time, he was working on a bus route. How do you like that? And every one he used started from Carfax, right in the middle of town."

"Marcus, honey, all the buses start from Carfax," Marge said. "Don't they?"

"Well. Most of them. But get this: There isn't one word in any of those newspaper reports about the cops questioning the bus conductors!" He sat back and lit another cigarette, looking very pleased with himself.

"Don't you think they'd have come forward?" Marge asked. "The British aren't like Americans. At least, they weren't then. They didn't mind getting involved, when it was a matter of justice."

"Yes, but bus conductors! It seems so obvious!"

"Well, if it's obvious to you, I'm sure it was obvious to the police," Marge said. "Maybe they questioned them and they didn't have anything to say, so it just didn't get into the papers. Besides, what are you going to do about it? You can't just go ask them. Not now."

"True." Marcus looked into his beer with ludicrous disappointment. "I keep forgetting how long ago it is. Seems like last month, sometimes."

"Twenty years, Marc." Marge took a sip of her own beer, set it down in the ring it had made on the plastic surface of the table. "Or do you think the police were covering something up?"

He shook his head. "No. Not that. I'm just playing master detective. It's more interesting than teaching English novels to idiots. Anyway," he went on, recovering much of his verve, "what I want to do is ask you about the Boston murders. Maybe you can give me a little support for a theory I've worked out."

"Theory?"

"I won't tell you what it is, because if I do, you'll start remembering slanted. Isn't that what Rosie used to say?"

Marge frowned. "Rosie."

"Jake Rosenbaum. The psychologist. You remember, the twenty-minute man."

"Oh, yeah. I was thinking about him just the other day, only I couldn't remember his name." Marge tried to remember just when that was but got only an impression of yellow light.

Marc nodded vigorously. "Now, how about the Boston stuff? Just exactly what parallels are there?"

"Marc—" she protested. "Oh, hell. All right. Can I have another beer first?"

He pushed the hair out of his eyes and signaled the waitress without losing the white intensity of his question, his face tight. Marge wondered idly what made it so important. She watched the bartender fill two mugs. "Now," Marcus said. "No, wait, I want to take notes."

[106]

When he had dug some paper out of a pocket she gave him the title and author of the book in which she'd found the most complete description, and of a couple of others in which she remembered seeing passing references.

"I don't know any of those," Marcus said. "They must have a big collection at the public library."

"I told you, a hundred books. And it's linked with the County and the U. You can get anything in the state from them," she said, already regretting that she'd yielded to his pressure.

He "walked" her—his word—through the murders in Boston, questioned every detail.

"I'm not an original source, Marcus," she protested. "I don't have the police reports at my fingertips."

"I don't know why they have to be so damned *shy* in these damned books," he said.

"Not everybody has your appetite."

"Sure they do," he said brusquely. She wondered what he would think of her index card, flipping from page to page. "Now." He scanned the notes he'd made. "Is that really all you can tell me?"

"That's all."

"Well, it all seems to check out. Now let me tell you what I'm thinking," he said, again sitting back with a self-satisfied smile. "Dick Green."

"Dick Green? What about him?"

Marcus made a disappointed *moue*. "Doesn't he fit?"

"Fit?" She stared at him. "As the murderer, you mean? How should I know?"

Marcus leaned forward and held out his hands in a pleading gesture. "Well, look. These things were obviously done by somebody with an inadequate image of himself as a man. And of all our crowd, who fits that better than Dick Green?"

"How should I know that?" she challenged.

He dropped his gaze to the tabletop and raised his eyebrows. "He never made a pass at you, did he."

"No, he didn't," Marge agreed. "On the other hand, neither did you."

"An unforgivable oversight," Marc said. "Besides, I was married."

"So was I."

"Well, so why should I have made a pass at you?" he asked.

"And why should Dick? We aren't talking about the *late* sixties, you know. There hadn't been any sexual revolution, or whatever you want to call it. We weren't even into Viet Nam yet, or not by much, anyway. People our age still believed in happy-ever-after."

"Oh, come *on*, Marge."

"I did, anyway."

A short silence followed, during which Marcus made squares of the rings of beer with his forefinger. "O-o-oh!" he exclaimed finally, with a vigorous shake of his head. "But you know what we all said about Dick Green!"

"Sure I know what we all said about him. But who's to say it was true? Just because he didn't mouth off like the rest of you wise guys?"

"It's a pretty theory." Marc set his mouth. "He was right there in Oxford, living near Carfax. He didn't have a car, so he'd have to use the bus."

"None of us had cars," Marge said. "And the bus lines *end* at Carfax, too. This guy could have lived anywhere." She drained her glass. Marc put two fingers up and waggled them at the waitress.

"Now, about Harvard, you're going to have to give me better details there, because I was in New Hampshire and I didn't get down to Cambridge very often," he continued. "What was Dick like there?"

"No," Marge said. "I'm not going to go around prying poor Dick apart just because you have some theory."

"Poor Dick." Marc chuckled. "That's a good one."

I don't like Marcus nearly as much as I used to, Marge thought. She drank half of the new mug of beer, not looking at him.

"Marge, we're talking about a murderer, don't forget. One who killed twelve women."

"Fifteen," Marge corrected absentmindedly.

Marcus went still, his mug half raised. "Fifteen? Seven at Oxford and five in Boston. I get twelve."

Hell, Marge thought. I may as well tell him. He'll have it out

[108]

of me anyway, so I'd better get it over with. "Three in Kansas, too, I think."

Marc smiled, a tight, vicious smile. "And Dick Green was at Western Mo."

"I didn't say where in Kansas," Marge reminded him.

"No, but I remember them. Yeah. It was in all the papers. About 1967, wasn't it? Or '68? In the middle of all the protests, I remember that."

"Sixty-six," Marge said in a thin voice.

"O-o-oh, yeah." Marcus closed his eyes. He's going to have an orgasm, Marge thought, disgusted. "I do remember, now. One of them was right after the Richard Speck thing."

Richard Speck, Marge thought. I read about him. Oh, yes, the one who killed all those nurses in Chicago.

"That was a year for crazies, wasn't it?" Marcus added. His voice caressed the words. "Wasn't that about the same time that guy got up in the tower at the University of Texas and shot up a bunch of people? Killed a dozen or so before they got him?"

"I thought you couldn't stand blood."

"Oh, I can't, I can't. Menstruation was a terrible shock to me."

"If it happened to you, I can see where it would be," Marge said tartly. Oh, boy, I really have had too much beer, she added to herself. She looked around for a clock, saw one behind the bar. Four-thirty. *Hogan's Heroes* was just coming on: The bartender leaned against the bar with his arms folded, absorbed in the TV. He looked to be about Chuck's age.

Marcus gave her a disgusted glance. "I've got the clippings on the Kansas ones, too. I know I do. I'll hunt them out tonight and study up on them. And I'll make you a little bet."

"What's that?"

"Dick Green's our boy."

Marge looked past him. A bluish streak of daylight illuminated the wall as the first of the after-work customers came in. "I'm not betting on anything of the kind."

"Why? You know something you're not saying?"

"No," she replied, locking gazes. "Do you?"

She was the first to look away. "Marc, thanks for lunch, but I've got to get home. My kids will be wondering what happened to me."

"That's right," Marcus said in a meditative tone. "I forgot, you've got kids."

Make a note of it, Marge thought.

Marc looked around for the waitress.

"Excuse me, I need the ladies' room." Marge got up, slightly unsteady.

When she returned, Marcus had paid the bill and was waiting for her. "We've got to get together again sometime soon, Marge," he said. "I bet between the two of us I can figure this all out, complete with proof."

"You do that." She walked blinking into the sunlight and took a deep breath of fumy city air. In Jimmy's you'd never know what time of day it was without the TV, she thought.

"Like I say, my money's on Dick Green." Marcus turned toward the library, heading for the bus line.

"Just because the guy's a little different." Marge sidestepped Marcus's hand as it reached for her waist.

"Isn't that just what we're looking for?" Marcus turned the grab into a wave. "Now, look." He built his theory all the way to the bus stop. Marge paid little attention. She had only just realized that, somewhere along the way, she had accepted the idea that one of the people she knew was a murderer, and she couldn't think why.

It could all still be coincidence, or a copycat, she thought, mounting the steps of her bus. She was relieved beyond measure that she wouldn't have to share it with Marcus.

By the time she got off the bus, she was feeling a little less woozy, but the walk home plunged her into an even sadder mood. Part of her wanted, badly, to believe Marcus's silly theory. That, she thought, could only be because otherwise she might have to believe it of someone else. Like Phil. Shoulders hunched, she opened the downstairs door.

She had barely stepped inside when the door to the first-floor front apartment whipped open and Mrs. Nemesis popped out. "Mrs. Brock," said the old woman, "after the other night, I really don't know what to think of you, really I don't, but I'm going to tell you this anyway, because I certainly don't want anything dreadful on my conscience." Her long pink nose, sharpened by years of poking into other people's business, twitched.

"What's that?" Marge asked wearily.

"Last night there was a man lurking across the street. I saw him distinctly from my bedroom window," Mrs. Nemesis spat out, nostrils flaring. "Since he can hardly have been interested in me, it must be you or one of those girls of yours who attracted his attention."

"What did he look like?" Marge asked, instantly alert.

"How should I know? It was dark. Why, Mrs. Brock," the old woman said, stepping closer, "have you been drinking? So early in the day?"

Marge held her eye steadily. "Yes," she said. "As a matter of fact, I have."

She climbed the stairs to her apartment with all the dignity she could muster, feeling those sharp eyes on her back, speared the lock with one stab of her key, and closed the door quietly behind her.

Then she went into the bathroom and threw up for the second time that day.

❧ XII ❧

WHEN Marge came into the living room, Claire was standing by the bookshelves, teasing a small spider that had built its web in the corner of one of the shelves. She was puffing her breath at it each time the beast decided it was safe to stretch its tiny legs out again. "Some lady called," she said. "Mrs. Lindstrom, or something like that. She said you'd know her, and please call back right away."

"Okay, I'll call her," Marge said. "Can't you leave that poor thing alone?"

"It's only a spider," Claire said, puffing again. "You okay, Mom?"

"Yes."

"I thought I heard you barfing."

"I was." Marge headed for the phone without bothering to explain. What could Julie want? Marge didn't think she could stand one single question more about the murders, not for quite a long while.

Julie answered on the second ring. "Oh, Marge," she said, sounding happy, "I'm so glad you called back. I'm planning a little get-together, just a few old friends for supper, and I wondered if you'd like to come."

"That sounds nice," Marge said cautiously. "When?"

"Oh, say this Friday, if you're free? Or we could make it another night, if you like."

"Julie," Marge said with a sudden qualm, "you're not planning this around me, are you?"

"Well, yes, as a matter of fact." Julie sounded disconcerted. "I've been thinking about what you said the other night, about renewing old acquaintances, and I thought it sounded like a good idea." Julie paused. "This way there wouldn't be any danger of anything, you know, like Sunday."

"Oh." Marge let every bit of her relief go into her voice. "I'm sorry, Julie. For a minute I was afraid you might want the details of the murders I was talking about the other day."

"Why would I want that?" Julie asked in a puzzled tone. "I like a good gossip as much as the next person, but murder! Really."

"I'm a little sensitive on the subject," Marge said, an oblique apology Julie would understand. "I spent the afternoon being questioned by Marcus Dellingham."

"Oh, you poor dear," Julie sympathized. "Isn't he a terror? He was over here on Monday, putting Kevin through the mill or whatever you want to call it. The fourth estate? No, that's newspapers."

"Third degree," Marge suggested.

"That's it, third degree. Terrible. He expects you to remember every little thing that ever happened to you in your entire life!"

"You don't have to tell me," Marge said and sighed. She stretched the phone cord to its limit and sat down on one of the kitchen chairs. Her stomach hurt, and she felt a little dizzy. "I just had a sample."

"Well, you know Kevin. He doesn't remember what happened twenty minutes ago, let alone twenty years. My heavens, Theenie was just a baby then!"

Marge blinked at her still-gleaming kitchen, discouraged. "I didn't think Kevin's memory was as bad as all that," she said. Am *I* planning to ask him questions? she wondered.

"Well, I'm exaggerating, of course," Julie confided. "But something about Marc makes you freeze, you know? He's so *positive!*"

"I know." Marge closed her eyes. They felt raw, as if she had cried all day. From the cigarette smoke in Jimmy's, most likely. The smell was stuck to her clothes. "Who else will be coming, Julie?" she asked.

"I hadn't really made up my mind. Do you like Dick Green? I know it sounds funny to ask straight out, but some people aren't very comfortable with him."

"He's okay. I knew him in Cleveland."

"Nice guy, yes. And Gwen Bishop. They're dating, did you know?"

Take that, Marcus. "No, I didn't know. What happened to Jack? Don't tell me they're divorced, too?"

Julie was silent for a moment. "Jack was killed in Viet Nam, Marge. You didn't know?"

"No." Marge, too, fell silent. A quiet, gentle guy, Jack. Hard even to imagine him in uniform.

"Well," Julie said briskly, "I haven't really thought much further. Phil, of course?"

"I—" Marge floundered. What could she say? I'm beginning to think he's very attractive, but unfortunately he got dressed up in a ski mask and attacked me last night?

"He's not a steady date, then?"

"No. Just Sunday, and lunch, once."

"Well. We'll see. *Not* the Dellinghams. That Debra is a vapid little thing, and right at the moment I don't care if I never see Marcus again."

"That bad?"

"That bad," Julie crackled. "Almost accused Kevin of murder straight out. I mean, really—Kevin!"

"He was on about Dick Green this afternoon, if it's any comfort," Marge said.

A brittle laugh came over the wire. "He would! Maybe Marc did it himself," Julie said darkly. "And we're being treated to one of his little theatricals, to deflect suspicion. I wouldn't put it past him. Can I count on you for Friday?"

"Yes, I can make it. What time?"

"Seven?"

"Fine. Which bus is closest, Julie?"

"Bus! Forget it. If I can't get Phil, I'll be sure to find you a ride. I'll get back to you, Marge."

Hanging up, Marge went back to the living room and curled up on the end of the couch.

"Do spiders get neurotic?" Claire asked.

"That one may. Why don't you leave it alone?"

Claire wiped the tiny web away with one forefinger and watched the spider lower itself to the floor. Amazing, Marge thought, that such a tiny body could hold enough whatever it was to spin such a long thread. Claire squished it.

"That takes care of that," she said, wiping her finger on the back of her pants. Marge looked at the tiny damp spot on the wood floor, vaguely disturbed.

"Anything to snack on in this house?" Claire asked.

"Popcorn."

Claire heaved a sigh, the extravagant sigh only a twelve-year-old can manage. "I guess I'll have to make my own," she said, pouting. She picked up the dustcloth she had been using before the spider distracted her and gave the shelf a halfhearted swipe.

"Where's Chuck, by the way?"

"Down at the playground with Gary Kowalsky and his basketball, showing off for all those preppy girls who play tennis," Claire said and sneered. "Fat chance either of them has." She went into the kitchen and began banging pans, getting out the big pot they used to make popcorn.

Marge leaned her head against the back of the couch and closed her eyes. Tomorrow, she promised herself, I will sleep very, very late.

"Mom, wake up!"

Marge opened her eyes. Could she really have slept? "What's the matter, Peg?"

"What's this story about some guy standing across the street all night, and Mrs. Nemesis told you about it, but you were in no condition to understand the urgency of the situation? She made it sound as if you were falling-down drunk in the middle of the afternoon!"

"I met an old friend and had a couple of beers," Marge said. "And I understood her perfectly. Somebody was lurking across the street. Last night."

"Aren't you upset?"

"No. Concerned. But what does she expect me to do about it, put on my deerstalker and take my magnifying glass across the street to see if he left any footprints on a concrete sidewalk?" Marge yawned. "I'd better do something about dinner," she said, standing up. "It's back to ground turkey and rice tonight."

"Where's Phil?"

"I have no idea."

"Oh." Peggy stood irresolutely in the doorway. "Sorry. If sorry's called for."

"I don't know, Peg," Marge said, yawning. "Nothing is making much sense the past few days. I wish I'd never taken that stupid job."

"Are you done with it already?"

"I've been fired," Marge said. "Laid off, I guess I should say. It was getting a little livelier than Phil's father liked."

"You think that man has anything to do with it?" Peggy asked. A couple of worry lines sprang up on her forehead. "The one Mrs. Nemesis saw?"

"Could."

"What'll we do?"

"We'll keep an eye out, and if we see him ourselves, we'll call the cops." Marge sounded much more reassuring than she felt.

"Maybe he'll fire-bomb the place," Claire suggested from in front of the TV.

"You watch too much television," Peggy snapped. She picked up the empty popcorn bowl from the floor next to Claire.

"It's only *TicTacDough*," Claire said. "They don't fire-bomb anybody on that. Hey! Maybe he's got a dragon and he's waiting for somebody to open the door so he can sic it on us!"

"You're the one who's sick," Peggy said. Marge left them arguing and went out to the kitchen to see what she could do with rice and turkey. Something quick—it was nearly seven.

And what would she do if Julie did get Phil to come to her supper? Marge stirred some frozen chopped onion into hot oil in the big iron pan, standing back from the spatters. Well, she comforted herself, Friday's two days away, and the way things have been happening lately, two days is a long, long time.

She woke early, not late, to the sound of wild geese honking low above the roof. Another sound, too: Peggy talking quietly. Marge listened, but she couldn't make out any words. Then she heard the receiver click back onto its hook and Peggy padding back down the hall to her room.

"Peggy?" she called softly.

Her daughter appeared, wraithlike in her pale flannel nightgown, in the darkened doorway. "I didn't know you were awake," she said. "Did the phone wake you?"

"I guess. I didn't hear it, though, only the geese going over."
The room was chilly, Marge noticed. Just a few more days of daylight savings time. She'd have to remind Mandelbaum to put up the storm windows this weekend.

"That was Mr. Greyborn," Peggy said. "He had bad news. Phil's been arrested."

"He has." Her voice sounded dull in her own ears, as if nothing was left in her to make it resonate. "What's it about?"

"I don't know. I told Mr. Greyborn I'd have you call him when you woke up. Why don't you sleep a little longer and call him at a more reasonable hour? It's only five."

No wonder it was so dark. "Okay, I'll do that," Marge said, turning onto her side.

"I'm going back to bed."

The pale shape disappeared, and a moment or two later Marge heard the springs creak in Peggy's bed. Another flight of migrating geese passed over the house, heading for one of the nearby lakes to rest for the day. Marge turned on her back.

Phil arrested. For the attack on her? How would they have found him so quickly? Her mouth twisted as she remembered him sitting at her kitchen table, telling her how efficient the police were at their job. Ironic.

Unless, of course, it had nothing to do with her. Was more serious. There was Sandra Jane Foster.

But could a man murder on Saturday night, then take a date to a party on Sunday, behaving perfectly normally? Wouldn't he be nervous, at least? A man would have to be crazy not to let it bother him. Crazier than she could quite believe Phil to be, for all his cops and robbers games.

Though, of course, she'd been insensitive before, and to her own husband. If she hadn't come down with VD, she'd never have suspected that Charles was sleeping with somebody else. Her ears burned with remembered shame.

"Don't take it so seriously," her lawyer had advised. "Hang on a bit, and he'll probably settle back down. You have your kids to think of. A lot of men go through this at about this point in the marriage. They're getting older, they think they're missing something—last fling of youth, you understand..."

She could picture the man, a fatherly type with pale, white-lashed blue eyes. He'd thought she was nuts, not accepting, not waiting. But he hadn't heard Charles shout "Hallelujah!" when she'd finally agreed to move out, he hadn't had to sit endless hours on the bench in the VD clinic where anybody might walk by, he hadn't been threatened with the carving knife, he hadn't felt lost and betrayed, he hadn't had to lie awake in a half-empty bed and wonder, what's wrong with me that my husband would rather make love to somebody else?

And he hadn't had to wonder if maybe the reason was that the act was more successful, more satisfying in that other bed.

Charles had had plenty of opportunity, too, she could see that now. Traveling gave a man a lot of openings, a freedom he hadn't had when he was teaching, coming home to dinner every night. And *she'd* been the one who had encouraged the shift in his career. Thought it would give him more confidence, that the confidence would spread, make better the exact things it had destroyed. Talk about irony! Dumb. Dumb, dumb, dumb.

You've thought all this before, Marge, me lass, she told herself, turning over to sprawl on her stomach with her face in the pillow. Don't think about it anymore. Gone. Done with. Time to move on. Charles's own phrases, good for her, too. What's sauce for the gander is sauce for the silly goose. Exhaustion won then: She dozed off. She dreamed of a spider that somehow sprouted wings and flew after her, screaming.

She woke again when the alarm rang at six-thirty, saw that Claire and Chuck were up and getting ready for school, put water on for tea, made the morning oatmeal. What day was this? Thursday. Peggy could sleep a little longer. She'd wait for the other two to get out of the way before she called Phil's father.

It was quarter past seven before she finally dragged one of the kitchen chairs across the room and sat down beside the telephone. She took a deep breath and dialed.

"Ah, Mrs. Brock," the bass voice said. It sounded less resonant, scratchier than on other occasions. "I'm sorry I called so early this morning. I've talked to my son since. I'm afraid I had misjudged your, er, relationship, or I'd never have considered disturbing you at that hour. You will apologize to your daughter for me, won't you?"

"That's all right," Marge said. "What's going on? I didn't wake you, did I?"

"No, no. I was awake. It seems Phil was arrested for that attack on you night before last." Greyborn paused, giving Marge time to be ashamed of her relief. "I thought you had decided not to go to the police."

Marge sat in uncomfortable silence for several seconds before replying. "I was thinking about that stocking," she said finally. "And that girl."

"The Foster girl?"

"Yes," she almost whispered.

"Out of the question, I'm happy to say. Phil's mother tells me he was out at her house for dinner on Saturday night, nowhere near Wood Lake. A lucky thing, too. He doesn't go there that often."

Again Marge was silent, again with relief. She took a deep breath, letting the tingle spread through her. "What happens now?" she asked, eyes closed.

"I've contacted my attorney," Greyborn said. "He's going to try to get bail set and get him out. Then, I don't know."

"Was it Phil who attacked me?" Marge asked. "Has he actually said so?"

Greyborn said nothing for a moment. "It wasn't a question I cared to ask," he said at last.

"Did you tell the police about the stocking?"

An even longer silence. "No."

"Why not?"

"It wasn't knotted."

She mulled that over for a moment. "I don't see."

"I don't think Phil, and I guess it really was Phil, intended to, shall we say, make use of it."

"But then, why bring it?"

"For theatrical effect, perhaps?" Greyborn cleared his throat. "May I ask whether you told the police about the stocking, Mrs. Brock?"

"No," Marge admitted. "No, I didn't. I don't know why." She let the wire sing emptily for a few seconds. "Mr. Greyborn...let me know what happens? Please?"

He sighed, a whistling in the receiver. "All right. I'll keep you informed."

"Thank you." She hung up, blinking hard against tears, and looked up to see Peggy standing in the doorway, still in her nightgown.

"Did they let him go?"

"Not yet. His father's going to let me know what happens."

"But why would they arrest Phil? What could he have done? I thought that speeding thing the other night was all taken care of."

"It wasn't speeding," Marge said and sighed. "It's a long story. Have some oatmeal and I'll try to fill you in."

Someone rapped sharply at the apartment door. "Who on earth is that?" Peggy asked. "I didn't hear the downstairs door. Did you?"

"No." Marge got up stiffly and went down the hall to call through the door, "Who is it?"

"It's Elvira Finster, from downstairs."

Marge opened the door on the chain and peered through the crack. "What's wrong, Miss Finster?"

"It's that man," the old woman said. "He was back again last night, standing on the sidewalk across the street bold as you please. What are you planning to do about it?"

"I can't do anything if I don't know about it," Marge pointed out. "Why didn't you call the police as soon as you noticed him?"

"You're the one who has dealings with the police, not I," Miss Finster said, her pink nose twitching. She drew herself up and glared at Marge.

"Well, call me and I'll call the police, if that's the way you want it," Marge said. "I don't want him hanging around any more than you do."

"It seems to me that you could keep a better eye out, since it's you and your daughters who attract that sort of attention," Miss Finster snapped. "Instead of having me run up and down these stairs like a servant." She turned and marched downward.

"Try to think of it as being a good neighbor," Marge called after her and shut the door.

"What did Mrs. Nemesis want?" Peggy asked.

"That guy was back last night."

"Ooo. I wonder who it is? You think you might have a love-lorn admirer?"

"More likely to be yours," Marge teased. "Seriously, Peggy, sit down. I have an awful lot I want to talk about."

"It seems to me," Peggy said when Marge had finished, "that it might be time to start worrying."

"Start!"

"Like this dinner Friday night. What if they're trying to get you out there to, like, silence you?"

Marge pulled her chin back and looked at her daughter. "Maybe you're the one who's been watching too much television. What makes you think my friends are stupid enough to silence me that way—invite me two days in advance so I can tell anybody I please exactly where I'll be?"

"True." Peggy shook the teapot and poured the last, dark brown drops into her cup. "I'm just trying not to think it's Phil, I guess. I like that guy, a lot."

Marge smiled briefly.

"And so do you."

Marge nodded slowly. "You know, it could all still be wrong. There could be no connection at all between these murders and anyone I know."

"Mr. Greyborn thinks so. Phil thinks so. Mr. Dellingham thinks so. And now there's this guy watching the house. What more do you want?"

Marge stared blankly at the kitchen window, biting her upper lip. "Phil was at his mother's house Saturday night," she blurted. "When that last girl was killed. That's in his favor, isn't it?"

"His mother's house. Come on, Mom. What if somebody accused Chuck of murder?"

"Chuck!"

"See? You wouldn't believe it, not for a minute. And you'd give him an alibi whether it was true or not, you know you would."

Marge opened her mouth, but the protest died.

"What makes you think Phil's mother would be any different, just because he's older?" Peggy asked.

Marge got up and refilled the teakettle, lit the flame under it.

"Well, what about this guy who's watching the house? That can't be Phil." *See who those lights behind us belong to...*

"Why not?"

"Why *not*? He's in jail!"

"You don't know what time he got arrested," Peggy pointed out. "And I bet you anything Mrs. Nemesis doesn't stay up all night watching some guy lurk."

"I don't think she ever sleeps, myself."

"Still." Peggy stood up. "I'm going to get dressed. Want the bathroom first?"

"No, thanks."

When the water boiled, Marge poured it over the tea leaves and promptly forgot about it. The resteeped tea would still be sitting on the table hours later, when Claire and Chuck came home from school.

In the meantime, Marge took her turn in the bathroom after Peggy and embarked upon the day.

❈XIII❈

THURSDAY continued rather aimlessly after Peggy had left. Marge gave the living room and the bathroom an acceptable cleaning, and then, on a whim, got out the notes she had made for George Greyborn and attempted to organize the Oxfordshire killings by dates.

The first thing she discovered was that Marcus Dellingham's memory was not quite all she had accepted it to be. The murders had by no means taken place every four weeks like clockwork. One in each of the last three months of 1961 and the first three of 1962, then an isolated one (not a second series at all) in mid-January of the following year. But the spacing was not so regular as the "one a month" implied: the December 7 killing had followed the one on November 30 by precisely one week.

But maybe Marc was right about their all taking place on the same day of the week?

Marge made herself a little calendar on the back of one of her index cards and counted days: yes. Seven weeks, exactly, between the first two, then the one a week later, then four weeks, seven weeks, three weeks.

What about the one on January 17, 1963? Marge scribbled away, hoping she was figuring right. Yes. All of the Oxfordshire ones on the same day of the week. But what day? Tuesday, according to Marcus, and he might be more accurate about something like that, she reflected.

Marge decided to put the question aside for the moment and listed the dates of the Boston killings. Five of them, the first on May 21, then July 9 and 30, one on August 27, the last on October 8. Three minutes with the pencil told her that these, too, all fell on the same day of the week, spaced seven, three, four, and six weeks apart. But she still didn't know which day.

Marge chewed on the end of the pencil and stared at her two lists for a few minutes, but they told her nothing more. Sighing, she turned to the Kansas notes. September 29, November 10, and the one from the following spring: late April, no date given.

Again, the first two were the same day of the week, and she couldn't rule it out for the last. "Now what?" she muttered, running her fingers through her hair. She jammed the pencil over her ear, next to the bow of her reading glasses, and got up restlessly to look out the window. Over the rims of the glasses, the leaves of the maples that lined the street fluttered downward, making rivers of gold in the gutters. Too nice a day to stay cooped up in a shabby apartment, worrying about murder.

To be thorough, she really should figure out whether the day of the week was the same on all three lists. The calculation looked fraught with opportunities for mistakes to her unmathematical eye. Go down to the library after all?

She took off her glasses and tucked them into her purse. Maybe the library had some kind of shortcut, some kind of universal calendar. She knocked the notecards into a square bundle, held them together with a double twist of a rubber band, and dropped them into the briefcase. All she'd need, really, was the small notebook in which she'd figured her lists. That she put into her shoulder bag with the glasses, and, running down the steps, she was free.

It was just past two-thirty when Marge climbed the long flight of granite steps and dragged open one of the bronze doors. When she entered it felt suffocating to her, similar to walking into a cave, say, and then being left there in utter blackness, or in a mine shaft, dusty, dim, like something she had seen in a Welsh documentary from the 1930s.

Mr. Whitney nodded to her as she passed. On impulse, she sat down just one seat away.

"We missed you the past two mornings," he said.

"I wasn't here, no."

"But your, er, companion was."

"Companion?" Was Phil here, looking for me? she wondered, her heart lifting.

"Perhaps that's the wrong word," Mr. Whitney said. "I meant the young man who was here the other morning and seemed so anxious that you not see him."

"Oh." It's not reasonable to be so disappointed, she told herself.

"He was here yesterday," Mr. Whitney said. "And again this morning, but when you hadn't appeared by ten-thirty, he left."

Marge contemplated the old man's earnest face. Could he be mistaking a perfectly innocent action for an interest in her? "Maybe it's not me he's looking for, after all," she said. "He wasn't even here once last week, when I was."

"Perhaps unable. Another obligation."

"Maybe he only wants to read."

"In that case, he would read, don't you think? Not just sit with a magazine in front of him, staring at the door, and snatch up the magazine to cover his face every time the door opens."

Marge nodded. "That does sound odd."

"At any rate, he's gone now." Mr. Whitney gave her a kindly smile and unexpectedly patted her hand. "But now perhaps we'd best stop talking. We wouldn't want to disturb anyone, would we?"

Marge grinned, shook her head, and went over to the encyclopedia shelf to see if one of the volumes there might have some sort of universal calendar.

She found what she wanted in the first place she looked. It took only a minute to figure out that every one of the killings had taken place on a Thursday night. At that, she felt a flush creep up from her neck: the trip had been totally unnecessary, after all. Because one of the killings had taken place on the day after Peggy was born. And she knew perfectly well that Peggy was born on a Wednesday.

I couldn't have known the Boston and Kansas ones were Thursdays, too, she consoled herself. Thursday. Seminar night. Always something special about it: from undergraduate days, even, when she and Charles had both attended a seminar on the Age of Reason. For which I wrote both papers, Marge recalled. What a chump I was! Dweller in a dream.

The guy must have some fetish about Thursday nights, she thought. Marcus's notion of the sexual deviate sounded a little more plausible now. But who? And how was she to find out? She couldn't very well go to bed with them all, camera and tape recorder at the ready.

She rubbed the base of her throat once with her right thumb and forefinger, an automatic little motion, and put the encyclopedia volume back. On her way out, she smiled again at Mr. Whitney.

So, what *did* she have in return for her dollar-twenty in bus fares? The day of the week for a string of fifteen murders. She thought it safe to assume that the last one was the same day as the others. Thursday, a day with no special meaning except that she herself thought of it as seminar night. Not that she hadn't, and Charles hadn't, also had classes on Monday, Tuesday, or Wednesday evenings from time to time. So even she had no reason to think of it that way, really.

The weather was still bright, the air still crisp and invigorating when she walked past the corner house on her block, admiring the sunny chrysanthemums that spilled over the weathered wood fence. It was the police car parked in front of her house, which she saw when she looked up from the flowers, that punctured her fragile baloon of contentment.

"Nothing's missing," Claire assured her. "At least, I don't think so."

Marge stood in the living-room doorway and surveyed the mess. The TV was untouched—who'd want it?—the asthmatic old stereo still stood in its dust mark. Every book had been pulled out of the bookshelves and dumped, every record shaken out of its jacket to roll where it chose. The carpet was turned back along the edges, the cushions flung out of the chairs.

"My necklace Dad gave me is still on my dresser, and Peggy's is in her drawer," Claire said.

The drawers of Marge's dresser had been pulled out and turned upside down, the contents scattered. The drawer case itself stood at an angle to the wall, revealing a nest of dust mice. Her briefcase had been emptied onto the contents of the desk drawers, all in a muddle near the door. Getting raped must be something like this, Marge surmised. I feel violated.

"You just came home and found it like this, or what?" Her voice came out fainter than she expected it to.

"Yeah," Chuck said. "I came up the stairs and the door was standing open. I could see the mess from there, so I did like they say, I cut out quick and went across the street to call the cops. The guy was gone by then."

"That's a blessing." Marge sighed. "I suppose Mrs. Nemesis is in her glory."

"She's not home."

"Figures." Marge went out to the kitchen and hunted through the freezer for the half-pint container. The two hundred dollars Charles had sent was still there. She put it back.

"Cop wants to talk to you, Mom," Claire called.

She met him halfway down the hall, a man built like a linebacker with natural shoulder pads. She was glad he was a policeman and not some random stranger. "Anything you can tell us to give us a fix on this?" he asked. "Like, what time you left?"

"Must have been one-thirty, quarter to two," Marge calculated.

"Notice anybody hanging around outside, anything like that?"

"Not then." A little thrill started at Marge's scalp and ran down her spine. "There has been somebody hanging around at night. Miss Finster—she lives downstairs—told me. Happened twice." Marge let her eyes rove over the mess in the living room again. Hours to clean it up, she thought. All evening.

"Why didn't you call us?"

"She didn't tell me until the next day. And *she* wouldn't call you because *she's* a law-abiding woman who doesn't deal with the police."

The cop's eyebrows went up, two almost hairless semicircles in his bland brown face. "Found anything missing yet?"

"Not that I can spot in two minutes." She moved into the living room then, peculiarly unwilling, as if it weren't really her room, or as if moving into it would bring the incident home. "Strange."

"Got any drugs in the house?"

"Aspirin. A few cold tablets," Marge said. "Half a dozen Valium, maybe."

"They missing, the Valium?"

She blinked at the cop and went into the bathroom to check. No, the little bottle with the few pills in the bottom was still pushed to the back of the top shelf of the medicine cabinet. A trifle dusty: She hadn't taken one in months. Maybe I should now, she thought, listening to the pills chatter against the plastic as her hand shook.

"Still there," she reported.

"Anything at all you keep in the house somebody might want that's gone? Liquor, maybe?"

"Hnnh," Marge snorted. She picked up one of the couch cushions, tossed it onto the couch, and sat on it. "No." Her eye traveled over the scrambled underwear, the dumped-out box of maxipads, the notecards scattered hither and yon, and she felt the heat rise into her face. "Wait," she said.

The bundle she had made of the cards on the three similar series of killings was gone. Wasn't it? "A little pack of notecards, like those others, with a red rubber band around it. Do you see it anywhere?" Marge began picking things up and piling them on the couch.

"Notes on what?" asked the cop.

"Murder."

He lowered himself gingerly onto the edge of the cushionless armchair and flipped open his own notebook. "Maybe you'd better tell me about them."

She told him. Not quite the same version she had told Peggy. A little better edited, as she phrased it to herself.

"Oh, that reminds me," Claire said cheerfully. "Mr. Greyborn called." Chuck gave her a poke, but she paid no attention. "He said everything's okay for now—Phil got out this morning, but he's got a bad case of laryngitis. So he can't talk. He'll call back later, he said."

Marge nodded. Shut up, Claire, she said mentally.

"I don't think this is exactly an ordinary burglary, Mrs. Brock," the policeman said with a short, narrow-eyed stare for Claire. "I'd get a good dead-bolt lock for your door if I was you. And see if you can get your landlord to put in a solid door. Anybody could break out one of those panels and be in in no time. One good kick."

Marge took a deep breath. "I'll try. But he's more likely just to ask me to move."

"Or raise the rent," Chuck added. "Can I see if the TV still works? There's a football game on tonight."

"Thursdays, too?"

"Two this season," the cop said with a huge grin. "Great, huh?"

"Yeah, sure. Great." Marge picked up three or four books,

put them on a shelf. "I can clean this mess up now, can't I?"

"Sure, go ahead. We're done. Just waiting for you."

"Do I have to help?" Chuck asked.

"Only if you want to watch that game," the cop replied with a wink at Marge. She followed him to the door.

"Thanks," she said, jerking her head toward the sounds of activity in the living room. "How do you think the guy got in? Is there any way to tell?"

"Slipped the lock with a credit card, probably," the cop said. He pushed twice against the snap bolt with his enormous index finger. "Nothing broke. Like I say, get yourself a dead bolt. Harder to open."

Marge closed the door behind him and leaned against it. Somebody's scared, she concluded. Somebody wants to know just exactly how much I know. And I hope he found out: not much. Not nearly enough.

She went out to the kitchen, put the kettle on to boil, and dumped that morning's cold tea out of the pot, wishing again that Peggy were home.

XIV

"I can't believe that telephone is ringing again," Marge protested. She started to pick her way out of the circle of records she was sorting out.

"I'll get it, I'm closer."

"Thanks, Peg." Marge recrossed her legs and resumed hunting for the jacket to *Petrouchka*. She had already declined to participate in a market research study of dog owners, talked briefly to Julie Lindstrom (who had told her that Phil had a dreadful cold and couldn't speak above a whisper, so she'd asked Gwen and Dick to pick her up around quarter past seven), demanded a better door and lock from an irate landlord (sobering him considerably when she told him her request was on the advice of the police), and refused a wonderful opportunity to subscribe to any of six magazines she never read and didn't want.

"It's for you," Peggy called from the kitchen. "Marcus Dellingham."

"Oh, good grief." Marge extricated herself from the pile of records again. "I guess I'd better see what he wants."

Peggy handed her the phone and headed back to the living room. "Hi, Marc," Marge said. "What can I do for you?"

"I just wondered if you'd run across anything else to help us with our detecting."

Besides that you've got a crummy memory? "No, Marc, I'm sorry. I haven't even looked. I told you I'm done with that job."

"I didn't think you were serious."

"Of course I'm serious," Marge said, biting off the words more than she'd meant to. "A job is a job, Marc. I can't afford to go around tracking down criminals on a lark." Never mind that I'm doing it anyway. "I've got three kids to feed."

"That's too bad." Marcus really sounded disappointed. "I've got it down to nine guys now. I was hoping you could help me eliminate some of them."

Nine? A fluttery feeling Marge recognized as panic spread

through her abdomen. Who were the other four? Or five, since Marcus wouldn't count himself? "You're giving up on Dick Green, then, I take it," she probed.

"Oh, no. He's still at the top of the list. And a few of them are doubtful, since I can't put them in Kansas at the right times. You sure you can't help?"

"Sorry, Marcus, no."

"What if I come over tonight?"

Was she imagining the caress in his voice? Marge thought not. "Not tonight, Marc. We had a burglary today and we're trying to get our stuff sorted out."

"A burglary! Marge, I bet this is just what we've been hoping for!"

"You don't have to sound so gleeful about it," Marge objected. "And I hate to disappoint you, but it was just some kids looking for cash and drugs."

"Oh. You lose much?"

"I don't have anything worth taking," Marge said. "Marc, I've got to get back to work if I want to sleep tonight, okay?"

She hung up, frowning, wondering why she had lied to him. And so smoothly, as if she had it worked out in advance!

Every fourth Tuesday.

Tossed off, just like that. Did he really misremember? Or was Tuesday a night he could account for, and Thursday a night when no one would know where he'd been? If he's studied those clippings, Marge reflected, he must know the actual dates by now, must know they're not what he said. But he didn't tell me. Why? Could he be testing me, somehow?

"I'm putting the record jackets in alphabetical order, Mom," Peggy said. "That way we can find the one we want and just stick the record in."

"Good idea."

"It's almost game time," Chuck said anxiously. "We gonna be done in time?"

Marge glanced about the room. "Looks like another hour's worth, Chuck. I don't see why the TV can't be on, though. You got any homework?"

"Just a little algebra. I can do it during the ads."

Marge tilted her head at her son.

"Okay, okay, I'll do it now." Chuck stalked out of the room, and Marge turned to the bookshelves to see if Claire had put everything back in order.

Anybody in that seminar Charles had taken at Oxford would be eliminated, Marge realized suddenly. It always ran late, until after the pubs closed, often until after the buses stopped running. Usually he'd caught a ride home with somebody, but once he'd had to walk, getting home chilled and surly. Marge put her hand on the spine of the book that had reminded her of the seminar: Wittgenstein's *Tractatus Logico-Philosophicus*. It had been a brand-new translation then, bought because she didn't read German.

And that seminar met on Thursdays, that she was sure of. During the murders. The bright-red binding of the book was stained, she remembered: breast milk, splashed on the front cover when Peggy was nursing and lost the nipple as Marge reached for the book, dating it as effectively as if it had been rubber-stamped at the library. She'd ask Charles who else was in that seminar the next time she talked to him.

Which reminded her, she was supposed to be finding a time when he could see all the kids at once.

He called in the middle of the next morning, from a pay phone. She could hear echoing footsteps in the background and the intermittent squeal of a door. "There you are," he said. "Did you find a time to get the kids together?"

"What about Sunday afternoon?"

"What about tonight?" Charles countered.

"Peggy's working tonight, Claire's going to be out baby-sitting, I'll be out, and I think Chuck is planning to go to the movies."

"Tomorrow, then."

"I didn't even ask about tomorrow," Marge said. "I thought you'd be busy on a Saturday."

"Considerate of you. Doesn't happen to be true."

"Well, I can ask," Marge offered. "They aren't home now, of course—Chuck and Claire are in school, and Peggy's working."

"Oh, leave it at Sunday, then," Charles sighed. "I can't keep piddling around."

"You didn't leave much of the week," Marge pointed out. "If you don't call until Friday morning, there's not much I can do about it."

"Yeah, yeah."

"Charles? Don't hang up, I want to ask you something."

"If it's about last Sunday, I already said I'm sorry."

"No. Oh, thanks for the money. We can use it. No, it's about that seminar, remember? The one you took at Oxford, on Wittgenstein?"

"It's not coming back to me," Charles said after a moment.

"On Thursday nights. Peggy was a baby."

"Thurs—oh. Yeah. Sort of." Charles sounded cautious. "I haven't thought about it in years. How come you're springing it on me now?"

"You don't remember who else took it, do you?"

"Marge, that was damn near twenty years ago," he replied, sounding aggrieved.

"I just thought you might," she said, backing down.

"Is it important?"

"Not really. I'm trying to put together some things that happened in 1961."

Charles was silent for a moment. "That wasn't '61. It was the fall of '62. I remember coming home one night and hearing Kennedy yap about the Cubans."

Kennedy. The flat New England accent, after two years in Oxford, had made her so homesick she had cried. But they'd heard that broadcast in the daytime, and at someone else's house. "I don't remember it that way," she said.

"Marge, I'm not going to argue about the world's most boring seminar, twenty years ago. Have it any way you please."

"Thanks."

"See you Sunday afternoon, then. What time?"

"Oh, anytime after noon."

She went straight from the kitchen to the living room and pulled the *Tractatus* from the shelf. Right on the front, the four whitened, roughened splashmarks, just as she had pictured them. Nobody's going to remember that far back without a crutch, she decided. Useless to try to make them.

And the phone was ringing again. Five minutes later, she had agreed to a typing job that might bring in a couple of hundred dollars.

George Greyborn called just after Marge had made a lunch of warmed-up leftovers, standing at the stove and eating out of the pan, something she would never have permitted her children to do. "I'm calling for Phil," he explained. "He can't talk, and he's got an ear infection, of all things. First one in forty years."

"Oh, dear. Does he need help?"

"No, he's fine. He wanted me to apologize for him, for the other night. He'll call you himself as soon as he can get some sound out, if you'll let him."

"I hope he will," Marge said.

"He was just trying to scare you."

Marge surprised herself with a tender smile. "I thought maybe that was it."

"And me. That's what the stocking was for, to scare me. Once I figured out why it didn't have a knot in it, I knew it had to be him."

"Why didn't it have a knot?"

"He didn't know what kind to tie."

"Oh." Marge thought about that for a minute or two. Could be. "Tell him I'm sorry I hurt his foot."

"His own damn fault, but I'll tell him. I have a question of my own for you, though, or I'd let him scramble out of this on his own."

"What's that?"

"Are you going to press charges?"

"No," Marge said. "I don't see much reason to do that. But I have a question, too. How did they catch him so quickly?"

"Somebody saw him getting into his car with that silly damn mask on and got his license number, and the times matched. I don't know what got into him. He won't talk about it. Probably feeling like the fool he is."

"Well. Thanks for calling, anyway." Marge put the receiver back on its hook, shaking her head. What a crazy Phil was! But sensitive, she added. Caring. All the things Mr. Charles Nice

Guy wasn't, including a nice guy. Or almost all. She didn't know about his sex life, but it could hardly be worse than Charles's. Sighing, she gathered the pot and spoon into the sink, wishing Peggy were home to keep her mind from going around and around.

The doorbell rang that evening just as Marge was putting on her earrings. She hastily checked the mirror to make sure her slip wasn't showing and stepped into her shoes.

"Your ride's here," Chuck said. "Gee, Mom, you look nice tonight."

She flashed a nervous smile. "Thanks."

Dick Green was already standing in the hall. Another rather tall, brown-haired man. None of them under five-eleven or so, Marge thought. Couldn't one of them, at least, have been a squatty blond? "What happened to your face?" she blurted when she got a closer look.

"You could say hello." Dick's smile was abbreviated by the stiffened scabs. "Considering it's been ten years."

"Hello. Nice to see you. What happened to your face?"

He put up a hand to touch the three deep scratches raked down one cheek. "My next-door neighbor has this big, friendly St. Bernard puppy," he said, shaking his head. "I was out in my yard last weekend, planting tulips, and the idiot animal jumped on me."

"That must hurt," Marge said. "They look kind of red."

"It doesn't hurt that much anymore. If you think this looks bad, you should have seen it Sunday. That's why I wasn't at the Lindstroms'. I hear you were there, though."

"Don't mention it."

"Yeah, I heard that, too. Not like Charlie, is it?"

"He's under a strain," Marge said. "He's been laid off." She retrieved a sweater from the hall closet in case the evening turned cool, said good-bye to Chuck, and went down the stairs.

"Must be rough on you," Dick remarked, opening the door of his Honda for her. "Charlie being out of a job."

"Not particularly." Marge slid into the back seat. "Hi, Gwen, nice to see you again."

Gwen turned on the front seat and peered around the head-rest. "What's not particularly?"

"Charles is out of a job, but it's not particularly hard on me," Marge said. "You got a haircut!"

"Like it?" Gwen touched the back of her head.

"Super. I like you with short hair."

"So do I," said Dick, getting in.

I should do something like that, Marge thought. I haven't changed my hairstyle in ten years. Time to start over again.

"How long have you been in touch with Kev and Julie?" Gwen asked as the car crunched over the dry leaves in the gutter.

"Since Sunday night." Dick made a sputtering sound. "Yeah," Marge agreed. "Great way to let all your old friends know you're around, wasn't it?"

"You still working on your murders?" Gwen asked.

"No."

"Aw. Here I thought I'd get another good story, and you bugged out on me."

"You're as bad as Marcus," Marge said. "He's been running around all week, questioning people, from what I hear. I ran into him on the bus a couple of days ago and didn't get loose for three hours. Though he did buy me lunch, to be fair."

"He missed me," Dick said. "Must have me pegged for the crime, or something."

"Who knows, with Marcus?" Marge asked, startled. Yes. One thing about Dick, she remembered now. Every once in a while he'd say something that suggested he knew exactly what people thought about him and found it hilarious. Did that stack up as insecure? she wondered. Too bad Jake Rosenbaum wasn't living in town, too. She'd draft him as consulting psychologist—he, at least, was short!

Dick took a different route than Phil had taken, missing the sharp right turn and the traffic blend. Marge was surprised to see that they were crossing the river already. The Lindstroms didn't live that far away, after all. "I didn't get to talk to anybody but you and Marcus on Sunday, Gwen," she said. "Is Kevin as outrageous as ever?"

"Worse, if anything," Gwen said. "But he's smoother about it now."

"Practice makes perfect," Marge said. "I'll be on the lookout, then."

"Oh, it's all in fun," Gwen assured her, laughing. "You always were a little too uptight, if you don't mind my saying so, Marge. Don't tell me you haven't learned to loosen up yet! Life begins at forty, you know."

"I must have missed the entrance," Marge said. Dick negotiated the off-ramp and headed south. "Who else will be there tonight, do you know?"

"Just the five of us, I think," Gwen said. "I didn't really talk to Julie very long."

Should she say anything about Jack? Marge worried. Or would it spoil Gwen's mood? Or, if she didn't, would Gwen think she was heartless for not offering sympathy? Only it must have been so long ago.... Before she could make up her mind, the little car rolled to a stop in front of the Lindstroms' square white house.

Marge went up the short front walk just as nervously as she had on Sunday, and with more reason. Julie stood at the door to greet them, with a smile that Marge thought looked rather brittle. But the hug, the quick kiss on the cheek seemed genuine enough.

"You have a lovely house, Julie," she said. "I meant to tell you Sunday, but I didn't get a chance."

"Let's not think about Sunday," Julie said. "Come sit down. What would you like to drink?"

"A little sherry, if you have it."

Kevin took orders, prepared drinks, delivered them to his wife and guests, sat down. No one said anything.

Marge looked at her watch. "Twenty of," she said. The rest of them laughed, and as the tension evaporated from the room, Marge took a sip of the sherry, rather pleased with herself. The conversation turned almost immediately to Marcus Dellingham. "I never saw a guy who wanted to live in the past so much," Kevin remarked.

"Not even you? With your Elizabethans?" Gwen asked.

"I don't mean history past, silly," Kevin rejoined. "Let me give you an example." He settled more firmly in his chair, looked around the circle to be sure he had their attention. "It's like, once we went out to some stables near Oxford, because old Marcus wanted to practice his posting."

"I didn't know you two could ride," Gwen said.

Kevin gave her an odd look. "There's a lot you don't know," he said. "Anyway, Marcus came around one afternoon to ask if I wanted to go riding. So we take the bus out, and he dickers with the guy, and he gets us a couple of horses, and there we are. And I'm sitting on mine and there's Marcus, he has to walk around the horse, like they teach you in driver's ed, checking the tires—"

"Kevin, honey, horses don't have tires," Julie said.

"Well, I don't know what he was checking, but that's what it looked like. And he fiddles with this, and he fiddles with that, and I'm sitting there, and my horse gets bored and does a little foxtrot—"

"Not really a foxtrot," Gwen said seriously. "That's when they're changing gaits. You mean a box step."

"He was Chubby Checker inventing the twist, for all I know," Kevin said. "Whose story is this, anyway?"

"Yours," Gwen conceded.

Kevin took a long swallow of his martini. "Thank you. Well, Marcus is dillydallying, and I'm sitting there, and finally I say, 'Come on, Marc, they charge by the hour, and the clock is ticking.' So Marcus gives me this look, you know the way he does, and he goes around the other side of the horse and jumps up, and he's sitting in the saddle *backward*."

"Oh." Marge groaned. She'd been had again.

"And I say to him, 'Marcus, you're facing the wrong way.' And he says, 'You can look where you're going if you want, I'd rather see where I've been.'"

"And here I was jealous because I thought you'd really gone riding, and I'd missed three years of it for nothing," Gwen said disgustedly.

"You did get a D.Phil.," Kevin pointed out.

"Like I said, nothing."

"Somebody could at least laugh at my story." Kevin put on an injured look.

"Nobody's laughing at Marcus this week, Kevin," Marge said. "He's making a thorough pest of himself."

"Amen."

"Let's go eat," Julie said, "before my soufflé falls through the bottom of the dish." She led the way to the screened porch, where a table had been set. "I thought we'd eat out here, since it's so warm, and it's probably the last chance we'll get this season. Kevin, will you pour the wine?"

Marge sat where Julie pointed. The big dracaena was missing, Marge noticed. She decided not to say anything: she'd feel bound to offer to replace it, and that she just could not afford.

"Julie, this is delicious," Gwen said.

Right. The soufflé was delicious. The salad was delicious. The potatoes were crisp, brown, and delicious. Everything else tasted as if it had come out of a gourmet cooking school, and it all went down with wine that seemed to come from a bottomless bottle. By the time the party shifted back to the living room, Marge was feeling more than a little tipsy.

She had barely sat down when a loud clang came from the backyard. "What was that?" she gasped. Dick half started from his chair, Julie turned and gazed out over the porch, Gwen's mouth opened silently.

"Just a dog in the garbage can, probably," Julie said. "Kevin, would you?"

Kevin put his glass down on the table and disappeared through the porch doorway. In a couple of minutes he was back. He picked up his glass and drained it before joining the rest of them in the living room. Julie handed him the brandy bottle and started setting out snifters on the coffee table. "Nice dog," Kevin said a little blurrily.

"Why?"

"Put the lid back on the can for me," Kevin said, and plunked into his chair.

XV

"Remember that seminar on Wittgenstein?" Marge asked. "Did you take it, Kevin? I know Dick did."

"Seminar on Wittgenstein?" Dick said. "No."

"At Oxford," Marge said patiently. "Fall of 1961, into 1962. I'm not sure about the spring."

"At Oxford?" Dick stared at her blankly. "I don't remember any seminar on Wittgenstein at Oxford. Cleveland, you mean. I taught it."

Marge shook her head. "Not that one. On Thursday nights, at Oxford. I don't remember which college," she persisted. "Charles took it, and I know you did."

"Thursday was Tipplers' Club, Marge." Dick put his snifter down very precisely on the table next to him. "What makes you think I took a seminar?"

"Because I wrote the paper for Charles."

"I always did think you wrote his papers," Kevin murmured.

Marge glanced at him and continued. "And—forgive me, Dick, but this is why I remember—Charles got only an A minus on that paper, and you got an A plus. He came home just seething, and he said, 'Can't you do better than that skinny damn faggot?'"

"I got an A plus on a paper on Wittgenstein at Oxford? Marge, you're nuts."

"I *remember* it," Marge said, as if that should be enough to convince anyone. "I bet I've even got the paper I wrote for Charles at home somewhere." She and Dick stared at each other in tense silence. Outside, a cricket stopped chirping.

"Talk about keeping everything," Julie remarked abruptly, "have you heard about Marcus Dellingham's collection of newspaper clippings?"

Marge flicked a glance at her, decided to let her change the subject if it was that important to her.

"More brandy, anyone?" Kevin raised the bottle. He made the rounds of the snifters and slumped back into his leather sling chair, setting the bottle carefully on the floor beside him. Marge swirled the brandy in her glass. Drat. Why would Dick deny being at that seminar?

Unless, of course, he sometimes wasn't? And thought denying it altogether was better than reminding people of his occasional absences?

She looked at Dick from beneath half-lowered lids, frowning slightly. He touched the scratches on his face lightly with his fingertips, stroking gently. They must itch, Marge thought. After five or six days, they would.

The others must have thought of Dick's tulips, too; the conversation turned to gardens, and Marge began to lose interest. She'd better slow down on the brandy, she advised herself, or she'd disgrace herself in front of the Lindstroms twice in the same week. Neat trick, when she hadn't seen them for seventeen years before that. She asked directions to the bathroom.

When she came back, they were talking again about Oxford. "I never understood why the cinema invariably let out fifteen minutes after the buses stopped running," Julie was saying. "We always had to take a cab, or walk the three miles home. And sometimes we went just to get warmed up, you know? The movies were the only way."

"Pubs," Dick said.

"Oh, yeah, the Thursday Tipplers' Club," Kevin agreed. "How come you never came, Marge?"

"Peggy was a baby," she pointed out.

"I used to take Theenie along," Kevin said. "Julie was forever taking some night class in this or that kind of drawing, over at the technical college, and I was always stuck with the kid."

"Charming way of putting it," Julie said. She seemed restless. Marge wondered if they should be going.

"So, how come?" Kevin raised his eyebrows.

"I don't know," Marge said. "I never was much on nursing in public."

"I didn't mind," Kevin said. "But then, I had a bottle." He performed an exaggerated leer.

"Two of them, usually," Julie said—rather tartly, Marge thought. "One for Theenie and one for you." She got up and went onto the porch, peered through the screen.

"Can I give you a hand with anything, Julie?" Gwen called after her.

"Not really. I'm just going to leave it all here. I'll catch it in the morning." Julie left the screen and came back.

"More brandy, folks?" Kevin managed to pour into their outstretched snifters without leaving his chair. "Yeah, the Thursday Tipplers' Club. Thursday—thirsty. Get it?"

"We were all there, Kevin, dear," Gwen said.

"What you missed." Kevin leaned back and grinned at Marge. "I remember one night, Julie was out smearing charcoal on a naked lady—"

"I took a class in life drawing," Julie footnoted.

"—and I don't know where everybody else was. It was just me and Theenie. Beautiful October night, like this one. No kind of time to sit home waiting for Julie to get done with her coloring book. So I took Theenie out to a pub on Banbury Road that somebody told me had the best bitter in town. Just to try it out, you know?"

"I always liked mild, myself," Dick said.

"I never drank beer at all," Gwen declared. "Couldn't stand the stuff—room temperature!"

"Which was icy cold, except in the middle of summer," Kevin said. "Anyway, me and Theenie—Theenie and I, I should say," he corrected, momentarily putting on a professorial voice, "went out to this place, and we were sitting in the public bar as befits us blue-collar types, and I look across to the lounge bar, and who should be there, large as life, but our Charlie."

"Charles!" Marge exclaimed. "Charles never went to a pub by himself!"

"See what you learn if you listen?" Kevin asked. "And did I say by himself? He has this girl on his lap—"

"Now I know you're joking," Julie remarked.

"—little girl with a chore girl hairdo, what we called an Irish Afro later on, and the bazooms on that kid! I mean, she had a pair!"

"Kevin," Julie said, "you've had too much."

Kevin looked at her, a steady look, and reached for the brandy bottle. "I'll know when I get there," he said.

"Tell me more about the bazooms," Dick demanded. The corners of his eyes crinkled slightly and the corners of his mouth drew down a fraction. "I have always had an enormous interest in bazooms."

"Oh, honestly," said Julie.

"I mean to tell you, they were something else," Kevin obliged. "Like she was born with silver tassels on her tits, you know?" He made twirling motions with his hands in front of his chest, stopped when the brandy slopped out of the glass.

"Kevin."

Kevin barely glanced at Julie and continued. "And I'm sitting there with Theenie, my darling innocent child, and I'm wondering what I should do, you know? Should I go say, 'Hey, Charlie, long time no see, let's take our dates for some fish and chips'?"

"And did you?" Gwen asked. She had molded herself into her chair, her own generous bazooms turned toward Dick.

"Nah. I sat there and I looked at him, and I thought, Charlie, you schmuck, what are you doing with that dolly on your lap? In your place, on a night like this, I'd run on home and hop in the sack with old Marge."

"Thanks," Marge said, grinning.

"I didn't realize you were so attracted to Marge in those days," Julie said rather coldly.

"I'm not! I mean, I wasn't. I mean—"

"Keep going, Kev," Marge demanded, laughing. "I want to see you get out of this one."

"Yes. Keep going." Julie sat up straight without smiling.

"Aw, Julie, you know I never slept with anybody but you," Kevin appealed. "It was just a joke."

Julie stood up. "Anybody else want any coffee?" she asked. "I'm going to make a pot."

Kevin looked at Marge and shrugged. "Sorry," he said. He swirled his empty glass and looked at it, as if surprised to find it empty. "She's right, I'm running off at the mouth too much. Never could keep the damn thing shut." He got heavily out of the chair and headed for the john.

Marge let her head fall back against the couch. "Tired?" Gwen asked. "We'll be going soon."

"Little woozy, to tell the truth," Marge confessed. "I'm not used to drinking like this."

"Well, we'll have some coffee and go," Gwen said. "You don't take Kevin seriously, do you?"

"Not once I figure out what's going on."

"That's his dumb way of trying to make you feel better," Gwen added.

Marge smiled. "I know. 'Scuse me," she said, yawning. "I think I'll go see if Julie can use any help."

Thank heaven tomorrow's Saturday, she thought on her way to the kitchen. I will sleep late, late, late.

The ringing of the telephone jolted Marge out of a confused dream of nasturtium vines and nesting cuckoos. Yawning, she stumbled out to the kitchen and picked up the receiver.

"Hi, Marge, it's Marc again," said a cheerful voice.

"Marc, why are you calling me at this hour?" Marge protested. She peered at the clock in the stove. Just past eight-thirty.

"Oh, did I wake you? Well, time to rise and shine anyway," Marcus said. "I've been talking to Phil."

"At this hour on a Saturday morning?"

"Actually, no. I went over there last night, when I couldn't get hold of you. Marge, did you know the guy's actually been arrested? He's out on bail! And he's got a doozy of a cold. Hope I don't catch it."

"Mmm." Marge pulled one of the chairs out from the table and slumped into it. "Why did you call, Marc?"

"I thought you might be ready to give me a progress report."

"Marcus, get it through your thick head, I'm not working on that job anymore. Just leave me out of it. I'm going back to bed." She stood up.

"Sorry I can't join you," Marcus said. "Don't you want to know why they let Phil loose?"

"Okay," Marge said, sighing. "You got me."

"Seems our last victim, that one a week ago, had long fingernails, and there was skin under them."

"Marcus, everybody's got skin under their fingernails. Come to the point, will you? I'm tired."

"That *is* the point. Somebody else's skin. A lot of it, under the nails of one hand. And Phil didn't have a scratch on him, so they had to let him go."

"Are you telling me that Phil was arrested for that murder?"

"What else could it be?"

Marge toyed with the idea of telling him, considered what that could lead to, resisted the temptation. "Marcus, have you ever heard of slander?" she asked. She hung up and stumbled back to bed.

The little prism in her window was no longer reflecting the early-morning sun. Marge, wide-awake, stared at it as it swung slightly in a draft. Scratches, she thought. Phil didn't have a scratch on him. She tried to picture Marcus inspecting Phil's hide for scratches, failed in a flurry of giggles.

Dick Green had scratches. A sobering thought. Deep scratches, like a woman fighting for her life might make, and a silly story to explain them. Marge closed her eyes. She hoped it wasn't Dick, just so Marcus would be wrong.

Marcus.

Did Marcus have a scratch on him? she wondered. She could think of a way to find out. Marge stretched and smiled lazily.

But she couldn't do it. Not because of the moral question, though there was one, or that she was beginning to despise the man heartily, although that was a consideration. Mostly just because it had been a long, long time since she'd been to bed with anyone, and the plain thought of it scared her out of her wits.

❧XVI❧

WHEN she got out of bed for the second time, Marge put the thought of murder resolutely aside and plunged into an ordinary Saturday routine. Shopping for groceries was hardest: not the walk to the supermarket or lugging the bags home in the rolling cart, but walking past the meat counter, where the bacon and lamb chops reminded her of Phil, and the bread counter, where the croissants in the brightly lit case had to be walked past to get to the bread. The minute she had the groceries unpacked, she promised herself, she'd give him a call.

He beat her to it.

"Phil, you sound rotten," she said. Nothing like being candid. "Are you sure you should be talking at all?" She tucked a package of colby cheese into the back of the vegetable bin, where Chuck wasn't likely to find it, and closed the refrigerator door.

"Probably not," he admitted. "But I need to talk to you, Marge. Is what Pop said right? You won't press charges for that dumb stunt I pulled?"

Marge moved away from the refrigerator, to ease the strain on the phone cord, and leaned against the counter. "No. I won't press charges."

"Guys who feel adolescent do adolescent things, I guess," Phil said. His voice sounded gritty. "All I can say is, I'm sorry."

"No harm done," Marge assured him. "Not to me, anyway. But what's all this business with Marcus? About scratches?"

"I don't know what you're talking about." He coughed, a deep-chest cough that worried her.

"Marcus called me this morning," Marge explained. "Early— he got me out of bed! He's playing detective for some reason, and he says he talked to you, and the cops had to let you go because you didn't have any scratches? Something about that girl who was killed last week must have scratched the guy who did it?"

"The cops let me go because Pop made bail." Phil's sigh turned into another cough. "I don't know what kind of game Marcus is playing, but I wish he'd quit. He came over last night with a bunch of dumb questions. He saw me limping and asked me if I'd scratched my foot."

"You're still limping? Oh, Phil, I'm so sorry!"

"I won't wonder any more about your having the nerve to defend yourself, I'll tell you that," Phil said. "Bad bruise and a stretched tendon. I'm supposed to keep off it for a few days." His voice grew raspier as he spoke. She heard him sipping something. "Then he told me the afternoon paper had reported that this girl had skin under her fingernails, so he's going around checking for scratches," he continued. "I was so peeved, I coughed in his face, but I don't suppose there's any hope he'll catch this damn thing."

"Wait'll he sees Dick Green," Marge said. "He'll drool."

"Dick's got scratches?"

"Deep ones, on his face. His neighbor's dog did it."

"His neighbor's dog? Scratched his face? It was on stilts, or what?"

"It's a St. Bernard, and Dick was planting tulips."

"Is that a fact?" Phil remarked. "He planning to tiptoe through them, or what?"

"I didn't ask. He's dating Gwen Bishop, by the way."

Phil coughed again. "Snide remark retracted," he said. "Marge, I'm giving out. I'll give you another call when I'm feeling better, if it's okay with you."

"It's just fine with me." Marge looked into the nearest grocery bag to see if she'd left anything perishable in it. "Phil?" she added. "I hope it's soon."

Not because of groceries, either, she thought as she hung up. She smiled contentedly. Thank you, Marcus Dellingham, for all demons banished.

She opened a cupboard door and stopped with a can of tomato sauce half raised to the shelf. Thanks for what? She still didn't know if Phil really wasn't scratched. Can't you trust your instincts? Marge asked herself. Images from the TV news flicked through her mind: children and mothers, wives, even, like that woman whose husband stashed a couple of dozen bodies in the crawl space under the family home, saying, "No, it just can't be!" But it had been. It had been.

Ten minutes later, Marge was explaining to Claire why she couldn't supply eight gallons of cider for the Halloween party she and her friends were planning, and the dailiness of life had taken over once again.

Charles showed up a little before one on Sunday afternoon, remote and irritated. Nothing to do with you, Marge told herself. Remember, he gets that way. Happened before. Nevertheless, she was relieved when Peggy suggested that they all drive to a city park and walk around the lake. Marge pled housework, to let Charles have his children to himself, and sat down to read with the windows wide to the sunny day. What a luxury, to have an afternoon to herself!

Not fifteen minutes later, the telephone rang. "I'm going to tear that damned thing right off the wall!" Marge said through her teeth as she uncurled from the couch to answer it.

"Marge, it's Marcus. I'm mad at you."

Likewise, she thought. "I'm sorry to hear that, Marc," she said evenly. "What have I done?"

"It's what you didn't do. You didn't tell me about the ones in Ohio."

"The ones what?"

"Killings. The killings in Ohio."

"Marcus," she said, sliding down the doorframe to sit cross-legged on the floor, "I don't know what you're talking about."

"The series of killings that fit our boy in Ohio in 1969. And don't tell me you didn't know about it, because I found them in a book in the public library."

"Well, I didn't know," Marge said, no longer hiding her annoyance.

"Sure you did. You told me you read all those books."

"I told you I'd skimmed most of them," Marge said. "I think, in fact, those were my exact words. So you can quit yelling at me."

"Marge, don't hang up," he said urgently. "I want to bounce this off somebody, and I can't get hold of George Greyborn."

Marge put her knees up and leaned her elbows on them. "Okay, Marc," she said, sighing. "If you must."

"April 17 and May 22. Mean anything to you?"

"In 1969?" He made an inarticulate agreeing noise. "I might have had an appointment with my obstetrician."

"What?"

"Joke, Marc. I was pregnant at the time."

"Marge, this is no joking matter."

"Don't you have any newspaper clippings?" she asked.

Marcus seemed impervious to sarcasm. "Not for these, and I gave all the others to Greyborn," he said. "That was before... Damn, I wish I had them back."

"I'm sure if you asked—"

"Never mind. What I need to know is, who was in the southeastern Cleveland area in 1969?"

Marge tried to draw a breath, but it seemed to be stuck. I was. Dick Green was. Phil. Phil was. "Where were you?" she countered, when she had made her ribs work and had only the fear in her belly to contend with.

"Right here. I've been here fourteen years. Marge, how well do you know Dick Green?"

"He doesn't confide his bad habits, if any, in me."

"Marge. Listen. If I can put him in the Cleveland area in 1969, I've got him." Marcus sounded elated.

"And then what? You'll go to the police?"

"Police! Are you nuts?"

She let the silence continue, puzzled. "Well, what will you do, Marcus?" she asked at last.

"Never mind. I got carried away. Forget I said anything. I'll get my clippings back from Greyborn tomorrow." He hung up.

Marge pulled herself to her feet and cradled the receiver. Checking the calendar beside the phone, she found that April 17 and May 22 fell on the same day of the week. Could have been a Thursday in 1969. She let the pages of the calendar fall back to October. "Hell, Marcus," she said aloud, "you just wrecked a perfect afternoon."

The book she had been enjoying before the phone rang no longer held her attention. Dick Green. The man who had been in all the right places at the right times. The man with the three deep, inflamed scratches on his cheek, and a ridiculous story to explain them. The man who denied being at a seminar Marge knew for a fact he had attended.

But was that really on Thursdays?

She got the flashlight from the side of the refrigerator and went down to the storage area in the basement, dragged her old footlocker out, and opened it. After several minutes of searching, she found the paper. Yes, it had a date: February 15, 1962. One week before the February killing, as she recalled. Therefore a Thursday. She tucked the sheaf of typescript under her arm and closed the trunk, locked everything up, climbed the stairs. The grade on the paper, marked in red ink, was an A minus. No comments anywhere. She stuck the paper into a desk drawer and reluctantly headed for the telephone.

Greyborn answered on the first ring. "I think I know who did all those murders," Marge said without even pausing to say hello. "Can I talk to you about it?"

"Sure," he said. "First thing tomorrow? I can meet you at my office at eight-fifteen. Too early?"

"I'll be there," Marge said a little breathlessly.

"Oh, and Mrs. Brock. Thank you for sending Marcus Dellingham over with all those clippings. They look to be extremely useful."

"He wants them back," she said.

"Well, of course I'll return them as soon as I'm done."

"No. I mean, he wants them back now. I just talked to him," Marge explained. "He was annoyed with himself for giving them to you, for some reason. We've found another batch—or he has. Southeastern Cleveland in 1969."

"I was southeast of Cleveland in 1969, myself," Greyborn said. "Dreadful. Drive anyone to murder. Did he say why he wanted the clippings back?"

"No, he didn't."

"Hmm." Greyborn paused for a minute. "I can think of several reasons, none of which reflects too well on our friend Marcus, I'm afraid. However, I'll see you in the morning, Mrs. Brock," he continued briskly. "Keep quiet about what you've just told me. Don't tell a soul, understand? No one."

"All right."

"Don't go out, if you can help it. Call a cab to come here. I'll pay you back."

"Okay," Marge agreed. As she hung up, the downstairs door banged open and she heard her family trooping up the stairs. She met them at the upper door, offering cocoa.

"Here, I brought you these," Charles said. He shoved a bundle wrapped in green tissue paper at her.

"Charles, what?" She peeked into the top of the roll of paper and saw yellow chrysanthemums, smelled their marvelous tart perfume.

"I thought you'd like them," he blurted.

"I love them. Thank you." Marge carried the flowers into the kitchen. Charles followed and watched as she arranged them in a pitcher. She glanced at him from time to time, puzzled at his behavior: He roamed the room, sat down, jumped up, made another circuit of the kitchen, sat down.

"They're beautiful," she said, holding the pitcher up. "I'll put them on the desk in the living room, where they can catch the sunlight."

"I'll take them," he said, again jumping up and taking the pitcher from her. "You make the cocoa." He clumped down the hall as she got the can of cocoa down and pried off the lid.

When she carried the tray of steaming cups into the living room, the chrysanthemums were sitting far back on the left-hand corner of the desk, the only spot where the sun still shone. Charles had flopped in the old armchair. He was scratching his side.

"Fleas?" she asked, good-humoredly.

"Some kind of bite." He took a cup of cocoa, sipped, complimented her on it. When he left, at five, he gave her a quick hug, held each of the girls a moment, put his arm across Chuck's shoulders.

"Gee, Dad, you'll see us again, won't you?" Chuck pulled away. "You act like you're leaving forever."

Charles glanced at Marge with what looked almost like terror. "No," he said. His voice was calm. "I'll be around a few days longer. It's been a nice afternoon, kids. See you."

Two minutes later, the white Buick roared away from the curb, and Marge stood contemplating the yellow flowers on the desk. Her very favorite flowers: Charles knew that. She stared at them, suspended between the almost discarded hope that he wanted her back, and the fear that he might. The sunlight had left the window completely now. She moved the pitcher farther onto the desk, where a bump wouldn't knock it off, and shut the window. The afternoon was turning. A fresh wind had sprung up, and while the sunlight still glowed in the tops of the maples, it felt like rain was on the way.

By morning, the rain had come and gone, leaving a dark, chilly day. Marge stood at the living-room window, watching for the cab. It seemed absurd to take a cab in broad daylight, but she was tired, willing not to have to make two transfers and endure the crowded rush-hour buses.

A blue-and-white car came slowly along the street, stopped, honked. Marge tied the belt of her raincoat and hurried downstairs, the briefcase banging against her legs as she tested the outer door to be sure it had locked. The cab honked again as she started down the steps. "I'm coming, I'm coming," she muttered.

The cabby had more to say about ice hockey than Marge had ever dreamed could be said. She was glad to pay him off and run the gauntlet of cold wind to get into the blue Victorian house. Bellflower Press was deserted, its opaque glass door window only a grayish glimmer in the entrance hall. The hall seemed different, almost ominous, without an editorial conference in progress.

She knocked on Greyborn's office door. After a minute or two she heard steps cross the reception room, a bolt draw back. "Good morning," he said. "I'm glad to see you."

She stepped inside and he turned the bolt behind her. "What's that about?" she asked.

"I've had some threatening phone calls, last night and again this morning. I'm not taking any chances."

"Threatening calls?" She crossed the outer office behind him, unbuttoning her coat.

"Somebody wants me not to do this book." He circled the desk and sat down behind it. "I half expected to find my office demolished when I got here, but as you see, I was lucky."

"Somebody broke into my apartment the other day," Marge said, sympathizing. "I'm supposed to be getting a new door tomorrow, and a dead-bolt lock, whatever that is."

[152]

"My dear child, do you mean to say you don't have one?" Greyborn raised his eyebrows at her. "I suppose you've got a chain on the door."

"Oh, yes. But the police tell me I need more than that."

"You do." Greyborn put both hands palms down on his desk. "Mrs. Brock, I meant to begin by apologizing for, um, misinterpreting your relationship with my son. I saw you leave his apartment last Sunday night—in an all-fired hurry, I must say—and I assumed..."

"That's all right," Marge said, able to smile at him again. "You're forgiven."

"Thank you. It's Phil's own damn fault, calling me about those murders when I was watching the news. The very next item was about that Foster girl—redhead, missing from a bar, so on. It clicked, and I borrowed a car from my neighbor and drove over to Phil's to ask you some questions—once a reporter, always a reporter, I guess. You two took off just as I turned the corner. I tried to follow you, but that boy drives like a maniac and my neighbor's Ford was no match for him."

"Oh, that was you! I'd forgotten all about it."

"I didn't know you'd seen me, or I'd have mentioned it sooner." He smiled a wicked little smile. "I bet it had Phil hopping, though. Now, tell me your theory."

Marge took a deep breath. "First I have to tell you about what I figured out from the books," she said. "One thing is, all of these have taken place on Thursday nights, except maybe the ones in Ohio, and, of course, the one last Saturday."

"What are the dates on the Ohio ones?"

"April 17 and May 22, 1969, according to Marcus."

"Mmm." Greyborn opened the top right-hand drawer of his desk and rummaged in it. "Here we are," he said. "Little gadget for finding out the day of the week for any date." He fiddled with it for a few minutes, his tongue protruding slightly over his lower lip. Phil does that, Marge thought, with a rush of affection for both men.

"Thursday it is." Greyborn announced a moment later. "What's so special about Thursday, I wonder?"

"I don't know. For me, I always think of it as seminar night."

"How's that?"

"Seems like seminars come on Tuesdays and Thursdays, and the interesting ones are always on Thursdays. At least, the ones Charles wanted to take always came on Thursdays. That was his favorite teaching day, too."

"And Charles is—?"

"My ex-husband," Marge said, surprised that he didn't know.

"Oh, yes. So Thursday is seminar day. Is that significant, though?"

"Probably not," Marge admitted. "But let me go on." She paused for a deep breath. "I figured that the person who did all these might be someone I know, because I happened to be in the general area when they—when they happened. I know that's just an assumption."

"Not likely to stand up in court," Greyborn agreed dryly. "But we're not in court, and I'm inclined to agree that the cases are connected, so go on."

"So I thought about all the people I knew who fit that. With the Ohio killings, it narrows down to two. One is Phil. The other one is a guy named Dick Green."

"But Phil didn't do the last one, so let's eliminate him for the moment," Greyborn said, as if he were working a crossword puzzle. "Tell me about Green."

"We all used to think he was homosexual," Marge said. "For some reason, it was always a big question: Is he, or isn't he? Remember, we're talking about the early sixties. Things were different then. *Nobody* came out of the closet. Not if they wanted to keep their jobs."

"Not many, anyway. Right."

"Personally, I don't think he is or was. But he always was a little strange, and he was in the right places at the right times. Now, Marcus Dellingham says that this girl who was killed last week is supposed to have scratched her murderer before she died."

"That was in the afternoon paper, right." Greyborn nodded, arms folded as he tilted back in his chair. Is this me talking like this? Marge wondered.

"And Dick Green has three big scratches on his face that look about the right age," she said in the same persuasive voice.

"Ah." Greyborn leaned forward. "Did he say how he got them?"

"His neighbor's dog did it while he was planting tulips, he says. Dick, I mean, not the dog."

"The dog was probably unplanting them. So that's what you're going on? Opportunity and scratches?"

"No, there's something else, too." Marge found the paper she had written so long ago and pulled it out of her briefcase. "Charles took a seminar at Oxford. I—well, I used to do most of Charles's written work for him, and I wrote this paper for that seminar. When we separated, I kept it."

Greyborn nodded vigorously, got up and peered through the slats of the venetian blinds, adjusted them so that the street disappeared completely. "Go on."

"Now, I know Dick Green was in that seminar." She repeated the anecdote she'd told at Lindstrom's. "But he denies it. Now, why would he do that if he weren't afraid that someone might remember he didn't show up at all the sessions?"

"Plausible, I suppose." Greyborn fingered the old term paper doubtfully. "Tell me why you think he's not homosexual."

"He's dating a woman I know."

Greyborn tossed his head slightly. "May or may not mean anything."

Marge had a sudden clear vision of precisely what it might mean to Gwen if Dick were really a murderer. She felt a little sick. What was she doing?

"What color hair does she have, this woman?" Greyborn asked.

"Color hair? Dark, going gray. Why?"

"Just an idea." Greyborn sat in silence for several minutes, tapping his pencil on the side of his desk, while Marge let her mind go blank. "That's all you have to go on?" he asked.

"Well, I know it's no proof."

"Because, Mrs. Brock, I can think of other possibilities." He jutted his chin at her. "Has it occurred to you that you also have red hair?"

XVII

"Excuse me," Greyborn said. "Would you mind waiting in the reception room for a couple of minutes?"

Puzzled, Marge got up and went out to Miss Turki's desk and sat down. Greyborn closed the door to the inner office. She heard him moving around, and the door opened again. "Come on back," he said.

She returned to the chair she'd been sitting in a few minutes before. "Sorry," Greyborn said. "Not even Phil knows where my safe is concealed, and I wanted to get these out. They're Dellingham's clippings. I've got the copies at home." He held up the top page for her to see. "I wish he'd cut out the masthead and mounted that with the clipping, instead of typing all the headings. I suppose he didn't want to use a bigger sheet of acetate."

"Must be expensive," Marge said. "I never saw clippings kept that way before."

"Ah, well. We all have our hobbies," Greyborn said. "Now, mine. February 1962. I see the date on that paper you wrote is the fifteenth. Tell me what your life was like then."

"*My* life?"

"Yes. Your life."

Marge stared at him a moment. "Let's see," she said, deciding to go along. She closed her eyes and tried to cast her mind back. "Peggy was a baby, not even three months old. Winter, of course. Hard to keep warm, because we had just the one electric fire—electric heater—and we were forever running out of shillings to put in the meter. I couldn't always get to the bank, with the baby," she added defensively, looking up at Greyborn. He nodded and shifted in his chair. "And Charles was taking that seminar. A continuation from first term. I'd written a paper for that, too—got an A on it."

"Do you have it with you?"

"No." Marge tried to remember what she'd seen in the footlocker the afternoon before. "I'm not sure I even still have it."

"No matter. Tell me about when Peggy was born."

"It was under National Health, of course. My mother—my father died, a long time ago—my mother wanted me to come back here, to this country, to have her, but we just didn't have enough money."

"How long had you been in England?"

"Oh, since late summer of 1960."

"Well over a year, then." Greyborn tapped the pencil on the desk. Marge wished he would quit. "She was born in November? Was Charles with you when she was born?"

"In 1961? Not on your life. I was hardly there myself."

"I see. Her birthday is what date?"

"November 29."

"The day before the second killing."

"Well, yes. But surely they don't have anything to do with one another!"

Greyborn continued to fiddle with his pencil, saying nothing, for a moment or two. He sighed heavily. "Tell me about October that year. You'd have been what, over seven months pregnant? And writing the other paper, maybe?"

"Oh, yes. I had to write that one, because Charles wasn't there."

"Oh?" Greyborn seemed to relax slightly. He smiled.

"His mother died in the middle of September and he had to fly home for the funeral," Marge explained. "Then he stuck around helping his father clear up some business for a few days—they had a terrible argument, never spoke to each other again." She shook her head sadly. "He got back early in October."

"By, say, the sixteenth?"

"Oh, sooner than that. A Sunday. What were the Sundays in October that year?"

Greyborn consulted his gadget. "First, eighth..."

"That's it, the eighth."

"Phil tells me your mother-in-law was a redhead?"

Marge looked at him in blank wonderment. "Yes, she was. Why?"

"And the first killing took place on the twelfth." Greyborn ran his finger down the column of newsprint in front of him. "Miss Deirdre Sullivan, eighteen years old, found in the lane behind the council flats off Banbury Road, last seen in the Cross and Crown talking to a dark-haired American."

Marge stared at him. *A pub on Banbury Road... what we called an Irish Afro later on... the bazooms on that kid!... running off at the mouth... never could keep the damn thing shut....* "Could you read that again?" she asked, her voice very small, like a child's.

He read it. Nothing changed.

Charles.

Marge dropped her face into her hands, pushed at her temples with the tips of her fingers. *I'm sorry about Saturday night...*

"You know something you haven't told me?" Greyborn asked, his voice gentle. "I've reminded you of something?"

"There's a guy named Kevin Lindstrom." Marge gulped. "Phil knows him. That's where the party was last week. Friday I went back for dinner, and Kevin told this story about Charles in a pub on Banbury Road, with a kid with a chore girl hairdo on his lap.... I... Kevin tells these stories, you never know if they're true or not, nine times out of ten he's just gassing off...." She sobbed once, took a deep breath. "Oh, it could be. It could be. But I saw Charles yesterday. He didn't have any scratches on his face!"

Some kind of bite.

"Everywhere you were, he was," Greyborn said. "I noticed that you left that out before. I wondered if this Dick Green might be someone you had to believe was guilty. I'm sorry."

Marge clenched her teeth, her fists, her toes. "We'd better go through the rest," she said. "I'll try to remem—oh, I can't believe it!"

"Just a hypothesis, Mrs. Brock. A theory. We aren't proving anything."

"Thank you." Marge scrambled through her shoulder bag, found a tissue, blew her nose. "Let's look at the rest."

"You're a remarkable woman," Greyborn said. "I can see why Phil is so intrigued by you."

Marge looked at him stonily. "November, we've already said, I was having Peggy. Charles could have been anywhere."

"Including the Pheasant's Pleasure, in Headington." Greyborn turned over one of the acetate pages. "Early December, the seventh. You'd have been home by then?"

"The seminar...no, wait. That was the time he missed the bus and had to walk home. I remember, I was making him a cup of tea and Peggy wouldn't stop crying, he was furious...he scared me." She gulped for air. "I was pretty upset in general, then. Peggy was so new and so helpless, and my own mother was so far away, and she wouldn't come help because she thought it would build my character to manage on my own. She's big on character-building," Marge added with more bitterness than she had known was in her. "Actually, I think I was being punished for not coming home like she told me to."

"Mmm."

"I was twenty-three, but I was really only a kid," Marge appealed. "I had a very sheltered childhood. I didn't have nearly the smarts Peggy has now, and she's not even twenty."

"I understand." Greyborn nodded. "Then we go on until just after the New Year. Things going better by then?"

"During the holidays...I don't...oh." Marge closed her eyes again. "We went out with some friends. The Lindstroms, in fact. And some others, I don't remember who."

"Where did you go?"

"Oh, a pub. There was a girl there, a redhead, a little drunk. Charles said I should get drunk like that, show a little, um, I can't remember exactly what...." Not true, but too obscene to repeat. Marge brushed a hand across her warm cheeks. "A little life, something like that. We got into an argument, and he stalked out. He didn't come back, and the Lindstroms walked me home. Charles was back by morning, but I don't know when he came in."

"Could that have been the fourth?"

She drew a deep breath, thinking. "Could have been, I guess. The pub was in the east end of town."

Greyborn got up and chose a book from his shelves. He sat down and leafed through it, checking against the clippings. "That one fits, too, I'm sorry to say," he reported. He closed the book. *A Guide to Oxford and Cambridge.*

"Oh—" Marge put her hand to her face, pressed the hand against the side of her nose, felt a headache begin in her knotted forehead. "That leaves three, doesn't it?"

"We can stop if you want."

"No. I want to finish. February next, isn't it? And we know he was in the seminar, because of the paper." Marge looked up, smiling on the brim of relief. "So he can't have done that one."

Greyborn gazed at her with something like pity, and she stopped in midbreath, apprehensive again.

"Anyone could put an A on that paper," he said. "Anyone with a red pen. It didn't have to be a professor."

"*Fake* it?"

He nodded. A little chunk of her pride gave way.

"He could even have made the whole thing up, just to have Thursdays free."

"Mmm-mmm. I saw it in the catalog." Marge thought it over. "But no one else took it, except Dick—and I guess not even Dick."

"So nobody would have talked about it."

She shook her head. "We wives always talked about kids, and shopping, and stuff like that, anyway."

"We still have the summer to account for."

"We were in Europe," Marge said, her voice dull. "In January, we had a scare—I thought I was pregnant."

Greyborn smiled briefly. "Boston?"

"We moved there in the summer of '64." Marge's breath caught unexpectedly. "I was carrying Chuck then."

"There we hit our first difficulty," Greyborn said. "One of these —shall we say, cases—occurred in May."

"Oh, we were there by then," Marge said. "I was using 'summer' loosely." As a child, she'd surprised a mouse in the kitchen and picked it up by the tail. Looking for a place to put it, she'd dropped it into a milk bottle her mother had washed, ready to put out for the milkman. The mouse had run around and around the square bottom, beating the glass walls with tiny forepaws at every turn. Thirty-five years later, Marge thought she knew how the beast had felt.

"Tell me about that summer."

"Rough. We had no money. My mother wouldn't lend us any—

bad for the character—and Charles's father still wasn't speaking to him."

"Why?"

"I never knew." Marge thought over Charles's terse explanations and discovered they made no sense. "Anyway, I got some typing jobs, and a couple of times Charles came up with an odd job, a little money. After the school year began, we had fellowship money, and then we were okay. I typed. We made out."

"And the killings stopped."

"The killings stopped."

"And the rest of the time in Cambridge was happy?"

"Oh, yes. After Chuck was born in November, I got a part-time job, we finished Charles's dissertation, the defense went well—he can talk—and he got the job in Kansas. A good salary. We thought we were over the hump."

"With character," Greyborn said with a tight, triangular smile.

"Oh, I should have a cast-iron character by now."

"And Kansas?"

"I was pregnant when we moved. Not happy about it, but I coped. I miscarried over Thanksgiving."

"Three cases, two before your, shall we say, misfortune," Greyborn mused.

Marge sighed. "Yes." Sunlight struck the pages on the desk, faded, brightened again.

"April 27?"

"Is that when it was? He didn't get the raise he expected."

"We seem to have a pattern, don't we? Of reacting to stress, perhaps?"

She nodded. "Ohio would be Claire. That is, I was pregnant— I was pregnant every time we moved, except this last one— Charles had been turned down for tenure in Kansas—and again in Cleveland—and he resigned. He'd missed a lot of classes"— Thursday night seminars, she remembered with a chill—"and I think he'd have been terminated anyway." Marge rubbed at her temples, trying to loosen the vise of her muscles. "After we'd been there a year, he got the sales job. He had that up to now. He's been laid off, though."

"Ah." Greyborn was playing with his pencil again. Marge

watched it turn, tap on the desk, turn. She wanted to snap it in half. "Is this your home area, Mrs. Brock?"

"No. I'm here only because Charles got transferred. After the divorce, I just stayed."

Greyborn fell silent. Marge watched him, her mind blank, opened her own mouth slightly when he took a breath to speak. "Tell me about your burglary. It begins to sound significant."

"Nothing was missing except the notecards for the three series of killings I knew about then."

"*Nothing* else?"

"Nothing worth taking, I guess. I had a couple of hundred dollars Charles had sent, in the freezer, but that wasn't touched."

"In the freezer! I wouldn't have looked there, myself. And I've been writing about thieves all my life." Greyborn smiled oddly. "You should write a book on how to hide things."

"Somebody's already done it."

"Happens." Greyborn shrugged and looked down at his desk. He's been taking notes, Marge realized. "I've noticed that you use shorthand, Mrs. Brock. Were the cards you lost in shorthand?"

"That's right, they were."

"Not many men read shorthand."

"Charles does." Marge found herself nodding. "That should have told me, I guess. But it's so natural for me, I just didn't think."

"We're forging quite a chain of evidence, don't you think?" Greyborn asked.

"Yes," she acknowledged, sighing.

"The question is, what should we do about it?"

Marge gazed at a point a little below the edge of Mr. Greyborn's desk, where a dot of sunlight had made it past the trees outside and the venetian blind, wobbling as the wind blew. "It doesn't seem possible," she said. "I lived with him so long, and even after I knew about the murders, it hardly crossed my mind....I keep thinking about the good times...."

"Perfectly natural. Nobody wants to think they've been living with a murderer, a rapist."

"That's another thing." Marge swallowed the lump in her throat, felt herself blush. "That makes it hard to believe, I mean.

I can't see how he *could*. All the while we were married, with all the time in the world, he often—that is, he had trouble—"

"He was impotent?" Greyborn supplied, nodding with her.

"The least little thing—"

"You don't need to talk about that. But we do have to decide what we should do about all this."

Marge sat still, willing to let him decide for her, unwilling to say so. "We should go to the police," she heard herself say at last, as if someone behind her had spoken. She stood up and clasped her briefcase to her chest like a baby and started for the door. When she got as far as the reception room, she started to cry. A hand on her shoulder, warm and comforting. She dropped the briefcase and turned toward Mr. Greyborn, let herself be drawn into a tight embrace and rocked slowly while he whispered, "Shhh, shhh, it's all right, everything will be all right."

By that time she could not even have told him his name. He was just a human form, something alive to sob against and hope for ease.

XVIII

"I THINK," said the elder Greyborn some minutes later, "that if my son knew what I've just been doing, he'd be insane with jealousy."

Marge tried to smile and was surprised to feel her mouth move. She blotted again at her eyes with the wad of tissues Mr. Greyborn had found in Miss Turki's desk. "I know it's right," she said, her voice almost under control. "I can feel it, I know I'll start remembering things, it all hangs together, but I can't believe it! Still!"

"That's natural." Mr. Greyborn sat down on the corner of the desk, snagged a tissue from the box, and dabbed at the shoulder of his jacket.

"Sorry." Marge glanced at him out of the corner of her eye, embarrassed at having had her tears kissed away like those of a child. "He brought me flowers, just yesterday," she remarked.

"Phil did? I thought he was still in bed."

"No, Charles. Yellow chrysanthemums, my favorite."

"My God, woman! You mean he's still in town?"

"Yes, he'll be here for a while longer, I think." Marge tossed the wad of tissues into the wastebasket and plucked two more tissues from the box. "He's looking for a job."

"I had no idea he was still in town."

"Well," Marge said, shrugging, "he is."

"What time is it? Nine-thirty. Hold on, I've got to think about this." Greyborn cupped his chin in his hand and stared blankly at the wall while Marge lowered herself slowly into Miss Turki's chair.

"We've got nothing at all linking him with the Foster girl, have we?" Greyborn asked suddenly.

"He fits the description, sort of."

"So does half the rest of the male population of the metropolitan area. We need more than that."

Marge put her hands on the desktop. "I saw him Friday, and he was a little nasty, but nothing unusual. Then Sunday, you know about that, he was really outrageous. And I hadn't even talked to him in between."

"Suggestive," Greyborn agreed. "But subjective. Knowing our friendly police, hardly enough to glance twice at. You could just be a vindictive ex-spouse."

"Then I can't help."

"I can see they'll take convincing," Greyborn said. "I don't see any reason to put you through that. If I stuck you in a safe public place for a couple of hours while I prepare the ground, do you think you could bear up?"

Marge stopped fringing the edge of the tissue she had in her hands and wiped her nose with it. "I guess so," she said. "If I had something to do to take my mind off it."

"Good. You can go to the library. I'll drive you over. I have a couple of references I want checked for another book, and you could do that for me. No murder, just some guy who figured out how to get a computer to cough out a lot of cash. Could you do that?"

"Okay." Rudderless, malleable, it didn't even occur to her to question whether she'd have the expertise needed. She let Greyborn lead her past the dark offices of Bellflower Press, around the corner to the parked BMW, remind her to fasten the seat belt.

"What kind of car does Charles drive?"

"A white Buick."

"You don't see it around, do you?"

Marge twisted in the seat to look up and down the street. "No."

"That's a relief." Greyborn put the car in gear and pulled away from the curb. "There's a mirror on the back of that sunshade," he said. "See if you can get it positioned to keep a lookout behind us, see if his car turns up following us."

"All right." Marge pulled the sunshade down. The street was clear. "I wonder if it was Charles watching my apartment," she said.

"Somebody was watching your apartment?"

"Before the break-in. Mrs. Nemesis—I mean, Miss Finster, the lady who lives downstairs—told me about it." Marge sighed, remembered that she was supposed to be watching the mirror, saw only a small red car against the clearing sky.

"Didn't you call the police?"

"No. She didn't tell me about it until the next day, either time."

"Good God, woman, why didn't you say something about it to me? Or Phil?"

"It didn't seem like there was anything anybody could do about it," Marge said, lacking even the energy to get annoyed at his tone.

"The police could have kept a lookout for him."

"This is a Watchbird Watching a Watcher." Marge giggled. "Remember Munro Leaf?"

"No," Greyborn said. "You're running away. Try to keep your mind on what's happening now."

Marge glanced at the mirror. All clear. "I can't help it," she said.

"Come, come, Mrs. Brock. You've already displayed the kind of courage you can have."

"Not courage. Shock." Marge's head felt light, unconnected. Reaction setting in, she told herself. Her hands twitched in her lap.

Greyborn scooted to the curb, fumbled in his inside jacket pocket, produced a small notebook. "Here we are. These are the references I want checked," he said, ripping a page out of the notebook. "Don't lose that, it's the only copy I've got."

Marge tucked the scrap of paper into her purse.

"When you're done, if I haven't shown up, go to the main reading room," Greyborn instructed. "Read a magazine or something. I'll meet you there when I've got things set with the police."

"Okay."

Greyborn reached over and gave her hand a pat. "Take heart, Mrs. Brock. Life goes on past all sorts of troubles. Take it from one who knows."

Marge gave him a wan smile and got out of the car as a bus rolled up behind it and honked. When she got to the top of the library steps, she turned to look back. The little silver car was still there, the bus six inches from its back bumper. As she struggled with the heavy bronze door, the car took off.

Without so much as a glance at Mr. Greyborn's list, she headed for the open stacks. First she wanted to check on Marcus. But the small hope she was harboring quickly died: Just as he had said, the slender book she'd passed over in favor of some fatter, juicier-looking ones gave the details of the Ohio murders. Two redheads, college students. The mouse in the bottle. She'd tossed some bread crumbs to it, after a while, and it had sat in the middle of the bottle and eaten them. Nobody was throwing her any crumbs. She put the book back and ran her fingers through her hair, her red hair, and leaned her head against one of the shelf supports for a moment or two until her legs felt stiffer, then dutifully fished the list out of her purse and looked at it.

Greyborn had even written down the call numbers for the books. She picked up the briefcase and collected all three of them and headed for the reading room.

John Whitney had a newspaper spread out in front of him and was just pushing his glasses back up his aristocratic nose as she walked in. Marge sat down at the same table, two seats away, and opened the first book. The citation was accurate. She checked it off and started hunting the next.

"Mrs. Brock," John Whitney whispered, "that's the gentleman, over by the encyclopedias. See if you can sneak a look."

She nodded without looking at him, got up and took a magazine at random from the rack, looked sideways at the man Mr. Whitney had pointed out. He had a magazine raised to cover his face, but she knew the hands that held it. Charles's.

Stay there, George Greyborn had said. She went back and sat down near Mr. Whitney. Stay there. I never told him about the man in the library. Stay here. She opened the magazine: it was a Christmas issue, full of gingerbread houses and dimpled children with stars in their eyes. One was a little orange-haired girl, a lot like Claire at the age of three. The tears threatened to return.

The women had been robbed, she remembered. Charles had never had a bill from Blackwell's all the time they were in Oxford: That she remembered, too. A little late to be wondering where the money for the books had come from, one or two of them every month. Hardbacks weren't cheap, not even in 1961.

The women had all been robbed.

What kind of jobs were those in Boston, which he got at a moment's notice, told her about only after they were done, when he'd already been paid?

The women had all been robbed. Earrings torn from the ears of one of them.

Marge put her fingers to her earlobes. How many gold earrings had she eaten, dropped into subway turnstiles, dressed her children in?

A heart had been carved in the library table, just beside the edge of the magazine. J.K. and N.S., whoever they might be. Marge absentmindedly traced it with her index finger. Another thought chilled her: Where had the stockings come from?

The sensible way to buy stockings, especially when you don't have much money, is to buy cheap ones, always the same kind and color, so that if one runs you can match the good mate with another. And that was how Marge had always bought stockings. She jammed them into a drawer—tidiness is nice, but there are limits—higgledy-piggledy. An extra one, or one missing, would never have been noticed. She'd never kept count. *The wearer had been type* O. Her own blood type.

Marge put a shaking hand over her eyes. The one argument she and Charles had had, the one real shouting match before the big blow up, had been over whether she should wear panty hose. Laughing, she'd told the story a dozen times, since. Laughing.

Her back crawled, as if Charles had run a finger down her spine from across the room. Don't turn around, she told herself. Don't let him know you know he's there. Don't.

He'd been so furious when she brought home the first pair. That had been when? Before they moved to Kansas? Shortly after? Garters are sexier, he'd said. What are you trying to do, turn me off completely?

Never mind that stockings leave a cold gap at the top of your thigh in winter, never mind that the garters get twisted, never mind that one may pop loose anytime and leave you with a stocking suspended from one point and working its way around your leg, never mind the ugly bumps in your skirt, garter belts are sexier, and Charles needed all the help he could get.

She'd offered a compromise: pantyhose for when she went out, a pair of stockings on hand for when they made love. No good. He wanted, he said, to be able to imagine her in her garter belt anytime.

And, incidentally, have a drawerful of stockings to choose from. Marge began to feel a cramp in her lower abdomen, her body rebelling against her mind. A single pair of stockings was too easy to keep track of. And pantyhose presented other problems—also easier to keep track of, and what do you do with the rest of the pair once you've liberated one leg? Stick it in your underwear drawer for your wife to find the next time she puts away the laundry?

Marge turned a page of the magazine and examined a snow scene with total uninterest, as cold as one of the blocks of ice on the shore of Lake Erie that long-ago Ohio winter.

Don't look at him. Don't look.

She looked up at the clock over the door instead. Ten-thirty already! Where was Mr. Greyborn? What was keeping him so long?

The cramp in Marge's belly began to spread, to change to the familiar flutter of panic. The police would not believe him, she knew it. He'd spend hours with them, maybe even be "detained," while she sat here with Charles, waiting, waiting. And at five-thirty she'd have to go home, and nothing would keep Charles from going with her.

Marge turned another page of the magazine and looked at a picture of some revolting little cookies, just like some she'd made the Christmas before, maybe out of this same magazine.

I have to get away from him, she thought. I have to lose him somewhere, call Mr. Greyborn to come to get me.

She turned Mr. Greyborn's list over and wrote in her clearest script, "Mr. Whitney: That man is dangerous. I'm leaving all my things here, so he'll think I'm still working. It's the only way I can think of to get away from him. Would you mind very much checking my briefcase at the desk? Thank you." She signed her name and tucked the slip of paper under the corner of the magazine, stood shakily.

The briefcase sat open beside her chair. She left it there and walked casually out of the room, willing herself to be natural, be calm. At the door she glanced back, just once. Charles met her eyes.

Pretend you didn't do that, she told herself. She leaned the door open, walked quickly to the pay phones, dialed Phil. No answer. Dialed Greyborn. No answer. Of course not. What was she thinking? He was still with the police. I cannot go back into that room, Marge thought. Can*not*!

Instead, she hurried down the echoing staircase, pressed through the squeaking bronze door at the bottom. Steps started down the staircase behind her.

A bus waited at the stop. Marge sprinted for it, swung onto it without even checking the sign, and let some coins fall into the fare box. At the back of the bus she slid into a window seat on the street side and pressed her face to the glass, willing the driver to pull out. A moment later, the motor roared into life and she sighed with a relief so complete she almost fainted.

"You forgot your briefcase," Charles said.

He dropped into the seat beside her and pushed it at her. "You wouldn't want to lose it," he said. "It looks expensive."

"I got it at a garage sale." Her fearful, furtive glance showed him staring straight ahead.

He nodded. "You've finally made the connection," he said. "I thought it would come long before this, when Claire told me what you were doing....I thought you'd *know*....It's been hard on me, Marge, waiting, watching you when I could. But now you're running, so I guess it's almost over." He inhaled sharply and examined a small piece of lined paper he had crumpled in his hand.

"What makes you think I'm running?" Brave words, but her voice quavered over them. Marge closed her eyes.

"Who's this Mr. Whitney?" Charles asked.

He had the note. I should have *given* it to Mr. Whitney, Marge thought. It had never entered her head that Charles would pick it up. Too late now. "The old man who was sitting near me."

"How much does he know?"

"Only that he's seen you watching me."

"Too much, maybe." His voice was high, taut. If he had talked like that on the phone, she'd never have recognized his voice. "He couldn't identify you. He wears the wrong glasses," she said.

"Does he?" Charles sounded uninterested. He ran his hand down her thigh. "Since when have you been wearing jeans all the time?"

"Four or five years, now." As if it mattered. If I can keep him talking, she realized, maybe he will show me a way out. Was the dime she'd had out for the phone still in her raincoat pocket? "Oh, well. I can improvise."

Marge glanced out the window and felt her stomach sink. Not only the wrong bus, but also a bus that went to the suburbs by way of a gray, deteriorated neighborhood where even Charles might seem like a friend. And then long, green, empty spaces where only one person at a time got off the bus, and at the end of the line, what? Fields? Trees? Footpaths?

Charles fingered his tie. He was looking for a job, she remembered. All dressed up and anywhere to go.

"Peggy will guess," he said. "A shame."

"They'll catch you, Charles," Marge said in a voice even less recognizable than his.

"Charles, Charles. Can't you ever call me Charlie?"

"Charlie." Anything to keep him happy. "I told the man I work for about you."

"Greyborn? I've talked to Greyborn. I'll tell you what Greyborn will do. He'll check up on your divorce. He'll think you're a silly woman out for revenge for the hard time I gave you, and he won't think twice about it when you're dead, because he'll be scrambling to find some other chump to do his scutwork."

"You're wrong, Charles," Marge said, alarmed. "He's going to the police with the story. Now. This minute."

"Charles. I can't *be* a Charles, damn it! And you can't scare me, Marge. I don't scare easy, not anymore. This didn't work, for instance." He reached into his shirt pocket and pulled out a folded piece of paper, which he handed to her.

Marge unfolded it. The paper stuck to her damp fingers. A

carbon copy, she saw, of a typed note with an odd, exaggerated typeface. Dates: all of the killings. A number: $10,000. One sentence: Instructions follow in *Tribune* classified ads. "Where did this come from?" she asked.

"Come on, Marge. You never were an actress. You pushed it under the door at my motel. Where's the original?" He started pawing through the briefcase.

"I never saw it before," she said. She started to refold the paper. It escaped from her shaking fingers, fluttered to the floor under the seat. She reached for it.

Charles clamped his hand on her wrist. "Leave it." She sat back and he released her. "Who else would it be?" he demanded. "Who else could figure it out?"

"I don't know," she whispered through a dry throat. Her pulse started to pound in her head. "I don't know."

"You got about half of them," he commented. "I'm amazed."

About half! The bus was entering a shopping center, she saw. She lurched to her feet and pulled the signal cord. "The Mall," called the driver.

"Please," Marge called back. Her voice cracked. She didn't sound too sure, even to herself. What would be at The Mall? She hadn't been there in four or five years. But there had to be people, three or four others were getting off the bus, leaving it empty, even on a Monday morning. Maybe policemen, she thought. Policemen at The Mall. She hurried to the bus door, steadied her way down the steps with both hands.

"They close at eleven," Charles said as he came down the steps behind her. "Then what?"

Eleven! Dear God, twelve more hours! She'd never last that long, she'd be dead of fright and he wouldn't have to lift a finger. Marge's knees began to soften. Charles steadied her. Then what? she asked herself, not even realizing that she had accepted his time limit. Bus back? Only if other people also got on, she saw at a glance. If only her head wouldn't pound so! The bus shelter faced away from The Mall's buildings toward a vast, lifeless parking lot. She could see herself running, stumbling under the bored floodlights, nobody there to notice. And some car would be sitting there, throwing a shadow.

Stiff-backed, she walked into the shopping center, Charles a half step behind her. The Muzak was playing "Tea for Two." Charles began to whistle through his teeth.

"Stop it, Cha—Charlie, I just can't stand it," she said. He kept whistling.

Ahead of her, a long, tiled wall, blind display windows puncturing it at intervals. She hurried past them, her heart now pounding in her mouth, heading for the central court: people, light, safety. Charles matched her, step for step. The telephones in the hallway were silly little half booths on stalks, no protection at all. Shouldn't there be a cop somewhere?

Not that Marge could see.

In the courtyard, in front of one of the main department stores, was a fishpond rimmed with a wide stone wall that served as a bench. Unable to go farther, Marge sat on it. Charles sat beside her. Children clambered over the bench, trailing their hands in the water, squealing when a goldfish eluded a chubby, grasping fist. The bottom of the shallow pond was dotted with pennies and nickels. Opposite her, a toothless old woman had rolled up the sleeve of her dragged-out sweater and was fishing the coins out.

A young woman with faded jeans and a mass of black, curly hair sat down on the other side of Charles and squeaked a stroller four inches forward, four inches back, forward, back, although nothing rode in it but a blanket and a grimy plush rabbit. Once Marge had done that, too. Rocked grocery bags on her hip, jiggled empty strollers. Back then, she'd been married, to this man beside her. He'd bounced Chuck on his knees, the baby gurgling and grinning, passed a football in the street to a skinny eight-year-old who dropped it every time, watched *Sesame Street* with Claire. That was real. That was real, not this.

"Charles, I don't believe this," she whispered.

He looked at her, the look she had once thought was passion. "Not yet," he said, sighing. "But it won't be long before you do. It won't be long now."

❧XIX❧

CHARLES was talking, a murmur Marge had to strain to hear above the soft pat of the fountain behind her.

He was mulling over possible ways of getting her alone, possible weapons to use. She listened, fascinated, not taking anything in. He had a dozen possibilities all mapped out. Her heart hammered against them.

He stopped talking abruptly as a cop strolled between the fishpond and the department store entrance, a hypothyroid-looking woman with fat hips that splayed her gun out in its holster, a woman who would never understand what Marge had to say, who might even laugh at her and tell her to go home and get some rest.

"You always knocked me down," Charles said.

"What?"

"Just like Mom always said, the only thing anyone would marry me for was a ticket. You wouldn't even let me do my own work, just in case I didn't do it well enough and I'd miss the big job, the big money."

"Charlie, what are you talking about?" Marge asked. "You asked me to do it."

"Once or twice, when I was stuck. And then all the sudden it was always. You were all over me, Marge." His voice was getting high and tight again, as if he might cry. Marge had never seen a man cry, except in the movies. She stared at him with her mouth slightly open, wanting to reach out, pull him close, soothe him. "Trying to smother me," he said. "I had to get loose, don't you see? I had to get *loose*."

The fat-hipped cop stood fifty feet away. A little red light came on the walkie-talkie at her hip; she raised it to her ear and put her head on one side in rapt attention.

"I thought, if I didn't live with you, it would help." His voice skittered even higher. "And for a while—" He stopped.

Or was it just a portable radio the cop had? Marge imagined jump-cuts in a movie, from the empty hall where the pay lockers mutely witnessed Charles's tie tightening around her neck, to the cop listening to a country singer on her radio, the music getting louder with every cut.

She looked at her fingernails and thought about biting them. The cop sauntered out of sight around a mountain of green plants.

"I was always nice to them," Charles said. "Every time, I thought, this one I won't. But they always got me to kill them, somehow." He lifted his left hip and pulled his handkerchief out of the back pocket of his pants, wiped at his eyes. "I was *nice* to them, Marge. You know I can be nice."

"Yes." Marge's mouth opened. She stared at him. This was something she should understand. She didn't.

"I always hoped you'd love me someday, Marge," he said wistfully.

"I did," she said. "I did."

"No. You never loved *me*. You loved some idea you had. That *Charles*, nothing to do with me, or none of this would have happened. You loved what you thought I could do for you, maybe." He brushed his hand across his mouth. "And then you went and did it yourself, anyway."

"Charlie, what are you talking about?"

He glanced at the stroller, which was still squeaking beside him. The woman got up and moved away, shouting to a little boy in grubby overalls to come with her.

"You did it all. Like you had a plan. Marge the mother, Marge the Brownie leader, Marge who chooses the words to put in her husband's mouth like she lays out the socks and the shirt to put on for him every morning, stuffs his prick into her when he can't do it himself—"

"Charlie!"

"Makes her kids all by herself. You know it, Marge." He stopped, sniffed, wiped his nose, twisted the handkerchief cornerwise into a long, strong rope, which he curved into a circle and studied, forearms on knees, lower lip protruding. The flare of pity Marge had felt a moment before guttered and died. Shaking, she looked around her. The steps to the lower level were only six feet to her right.

"It's all your fault, don't you see? Those girls. All those girls...if you had only really loved *me*..."

Her hands crossed over her chest. She glanced wildly at him and jumped to her feet, dashed down the nearby steps two at a time, raced across the tiled floor with her joggers making tiny thumps like a beating heart, rounded the corner into the first shop, and rejoiced at the sudden silence of her feet on carpet.

She was in the game room.

She sprinted for the back of the long arcade and stopped with one of the old-fashioned pinball machines between herself and the open mouth of the room. The dim light, shifting, colored, was a friend now, not the gray, dark enemy of her fantasy of the hall of lockers.

This is not happening, Marge thought. Not to me. It's a movie. No, a dream. In a couple of minutes, I'll wake up and have breakfast and get dressed and go tell Mr. Greyborn all about Dick Green.

How quiet it seemed! Toward the front of the arcade, the space games whistled and whirred, sounds that weren't sounds. Nobody playing. School time. All the kids in school with their quarters in their pockets. Mothers with toddlers didn't come here to play Pac-Man and Space Invaders. One of the games emitted a few desultory bongs. Maybe she wasn't alone, then.

Charles rounded the corner by the stairwell, taking his time.

Marge pressed herself to the wall between two of the taller games and closed her eyes, then couldn't force them open again, not even to see if Charles had spotted her. This isn't happening, she thought again.

The machine beside her gave off a faint warmth. She cuddled up to it, numb, waiting. The game at the front of the arcade finished in a flurry of bells and the place was quiet, except for the enticing nonsounds of the electronic games.

Marge hardly breathed. Silence. What she thought of as silence. No human sound but her own heart beating. In the back of her mind, the pinball song from *Sesame Street* absurdly zinging, onetwothree *four* five, six seveneight...

"I can do it with one hand." Charles clasped a hand over her mouth. Her eyes snapped open.

Charles smiled, although his forehead was creased into a

frown and his eyes looked pained. "I'm sorry, Marge," he whispered. "You can see it has to be done, can't you?"

His other hand fumbled at her throat, began to press into it. The numbness left. She tried to struggle. "Relax," Charles said. "Relax, can't you? I don't want to hurt you, Marge. Please, don't make it so hard." His voice got higher, a dog's whine. The wrinkles on his forehead tightened. He was sweating. How could he sweat when she felt so cold? "Marge, *please.*"

She got her hands between his arms and tried to push them up and away, but he was like one of the robots from the games, steel and light and no heart. She kicked, felt the rubber toe of her shoe bounce off his shin. He shifted his feet away, pressing her harder into the corner between wall and machine. Suddenly her arms were leaden. Her hands dropped.

"That's better. I'm glad you found a corner," he said, panting. "It'll be easier, I think. I never did it this way before."

Teardrops of light swam into the dimness of the arcade, little pale blue fish edged with bold zigzag patterns. Is this what it's like? she wondered. Is this it?

"That's enough. Hands on your head. Turn around, real slow."

The pressure left. Charles straightened. Marge slid down the wall and hunkered next to the machine, coughing, or trying to. "No quick moves," the fat-hipped cop said, a voice like a whip.

Marge let her head sag back and took a breath. Her throat felt closed. "Step over here, please," she heard the cop say. "Hands on the wall, please."

Please, Marge thought. It takes a woman to say please at a time like this.

If the cop thought saying please was odd, she didn't show it. "Legs back," she ordered. "Farther. Spread 'em out. That's it." Two more police officers hurried into the shadows where Charles and the fat-hipped cop stood. Bright lights stabbed out of the ceiling, showing the dust, the threadbare spots in the carpet in front of each game.

One of the officers knelt beside her, touched her cheek. She rolled her eyes toward him, couldn't say anything, closed her eyes.

"Turn around, fella," she heard the fat-hipped cop say.

"Look at that, Jesse," said one of the others, falsetto. "You got him all excited."

"That's me," said the fat-hipped cop. Marge opened her eyes again, looked up. The cop gave her a mechanical grin and walked away, Charles walking slowly ahead of her gun, his hands locked behind him in shiny metal cuffs.

"How's your neck?" asked the man kneeling beside her. He did something at his side. Putting his gun away.

"I'll be okay," Marge whispered.

"We're going to take you to the hospital now, get you checked over," the officer said. "Think you can walk, or shall I call for a stretcher?"

"I can walk," Marge croaked. She got to her feet with his hand under her elbow and stumbled past the games. Near the front of the arcade, a kid of about fourteen looked up as they passed, went back to pushing buttons. The game bonged. He's been here all along, Marge thought, chilled. I was being murdered back there, and he just kept playing his damned game!

"You," said the cop, pausing. "How come you're not in school?"

* * * * *

"You were very lucky."

Marge smiled at Phil from the raised head of the hospital bed. "I know," she whispered.

"Pop went to the library to get you, and you weren't there. Some old guy told him you had left suddenly and a man who had been watching you left right behind you. Pop put two and two together and went straight back to the police."

"How did they find me?" Marge forgot to whisper, coughed, put her hand to her neck.

"That bus driver. Smart man. Saw you get on, saw Charlie talking to you, saw you get off, thought there was something funny about the way you were acting. Then he saw you'd left your briefcase—that was a very smart thing to do, by the way. I'm proud of you."

Marge shrugged slightly.

"Anyway, the driver also found that note you wrote to Mr.

Whitney and got on his radio to his dispatcher, who called the police. Who's Whitney, by the way?"

"The man in the library." She swallowed several times. "I hope they kept that note. It's on the back of something your father didn't want me to lose."

"Shame on you for losing it, then." Phil sat back and looked at her for a minute, smiling. "The driver found another paper, too. I haven't seen it, but I bet it looked like this." He handed her a fuzzier carbon of the note Charles had had. "Turned up in my mailbox this morning. Dick Green got one, too."

"Marcus." A little matter of ten thousand to fix up an old house, no doubt. So that was why the detective game was so important.

Phil was nodding. "Matches the typed headlines on his Kansas clippings, Pop says." He put a hand on her forearm and squeezed. "They won't let me stay much longer, Marge. You're supposed to rest."

She smiled at him and reached out. He took her hand. "And you're out of it with just a sore throat. Oh, Marge, I can't tell you how happy I am."

She shook her head and turned her face away, feeling more tears beginning to slide out from under her already raw lids. "That's the least of it," she whispered.

"Sorry. Stupid of me." Phil got up and kissed her cheek. "There's an old witch in a nurse's uniform making signals at me from the door. We'll talk more later."

The nurse, a pretty woman in her late twenties, gave her some kind of sedative. Marge closed her eyes and let herself drift. After a time another nurse came into the room. "Your daughter is here to see you, Mrs. Brock," she announced.

Marge opened her eyes on Peggy. "I'm sorry," Marge whispered.

"I don't understand what's going on," Peggy complained. "Who is Dad supposed to have killed? Why would he kill anybody? Why did he try to kill you? And did you know that—that—vulture is planning to write a book about it? Can you believe it?"

Marge felt her mouth grin. "I believe it," she whispered. "Tell him I want half the royalties."

"Mom," Peggy said, "I think maybe something in your head got busted loose."

"Maybe so," Marge said. "Maybe so." She drifted into sleep again, without intending to.

Later, it was Phil beside the bed when she opened her eyes. "They say you can go home soon," he said. "Will you let me come with you?"

Marge looked at the wall behind his head, a soft green wall like the hope of spring. "Okay," she whispered.

"This is going to be really rough on your kids," Phil said. "They'll need help. You know that."

She nodded. Already her neck wasn't quite so sore, or sore in a different way. "Especially Claire," she said, aloud. It didn't hurt so very much.

"I thought Chuck, even more." Phil sat quietly for a moment. "But you may be right. I don't know much about girls. Anyway, if I can do anything to help, I want to."

She smiled. "Feed them."

"What?"

"Feed them. Chuck likes sausage. He burned what you bought before. I'm not supposed to tell you, in case it makes you decide not to buy any more."

Phil blinked. "You know, Marge, I think Pop's right. I think you're going to come out of this okay."

"Someday," she said. "Someday, maybe." He stood up against the light from the window, much as he had in the library so few days before. A pleasant-faced man. He bent over the bed and kissed her lightly, the merest feather of a kiss, to which she wonderingly felt her whole body respond. She sat up and caught at his shirt, to draw him back down so she could kiss him back.

M
831189 √

Taylor

Footnote to murder.